THE STAKEOUT DIARIES

JON SMITH

BAL
KON
media

THE STAKEOUT DIARIES
Published by Balkon Media

Paperback edition ISBN: 978-1-916970-19-9
Also available as an E-book

A CIP catalogue record for this title is available from the British Library.

Cover Illustrations & Design: Balkon Media

ALSO BY JON SMITH

FICTION

The Fifth Horseman

Destiny Can Bite Me (Fang & Loathing #1)

The Stakeout Diaries (Fang & Loathing #2)

Rewrite the Dead (Fang & Loathing #3)

YOUNG ADULT

The Arb

CHILDREN'S FICTION

Toytopia

NON-FICTION

Once Upon A Brand

Founder Mode

The Bloke's Guide To Pregnancy

The Bloke's Guide To Babies

Get Into Bed With Google

Google Adwords That Work

Smarter Business Start-Ups

Start An Online Business

Digital Marketing For Businesses

ONE

In the Court of Pale Affairs, light existed only by special dispensation and with the strictest supervision. Torch flames guttered in sconces at two-metre intervals, doing their best to illuminate a chamber whose primary export was shadow. Everything that wasn't marble was velvet, and everything that wasn't velvet was lacquered wood, which meant that dust settled on the place like snow in a crypt. Vincent could hear Mrs Barley plotting a coup against a particularly recalcitrant dust-bunny even as the fate of his immortal soul was being debated two rows up.

He squinted at the dais, making a show of indifference that was only slightly ruined by the fact that his eyes kept watering from the torch smoke. At the head of the Council sat Elder Mortimer Blackthorn, whose cheekbones had been the envy of the Victorian death-mask circuit, and who maintained an expression of perpetual, disappointed grandeur, like a statue that had once been the centrepiece of a much better museum. He was currently intoning Vincent's name as if reciting an especially obstinate stain from a dry-cleaning manifest.

"Vincent Lupo, also known by the aliases C. Lowell, Anselm Grieves, and the entirely indefensible Lady Vivien Despot, you are summoned before this Council to answer for your latest episode of... disrepute."

Vincent inclined his head just enough to suggest "continue," but not enough to suggest "grovelling." Next to him, Mrs Barley pressed her lips together and made a tally mark on the clipboard she'd produced from the depths of her handbag. Ren, for her part, had adopted the classic pose of the condemned: hands shoved in pockets, shoulders hunched, eyes fixed on a spot just above the speaker's head, as if bracing for an incoming weather front.

The Council chamber was technically full, but as with most supernatural bodies, "full" meant that a number of its seats were occupied by effigies, standing proxies, or—as had appeared today—a particularly lifelike marzipan replica. Vincent counted five actual vampires, three whispering shadows, and a grand total of two mortals: Mrs Barley and Ren. He wasn't quite sure if Mrs Barley really counted as mortal in the strictest sense, but as she was capable of surviving more than forty minutes without a blood-based diet, it was easier to throw her in the pot.

Blackthorn continued, warming to his material. "The events of the 14th instant, Soho, have been brought to our attention. To wit: a coven of unlicensed cultists, operating within the Orpheum Theatre, was summarily dispatched with what can only be described as excessive force, leaving behind not only charred mortal remains but a scene so conspicuous as to attract the attention of the Metropolitan Police, two dozen amateur sleuths, and the entirety of TikTok's 'Paranormal London' vertical. Would you care to comment on your... methods?"

He let "methods" hang in the air, dripping with the sort of disdain usually reserved for cold tea and travel bloggers.

Vincent cleared his throat. "Well, Elder, if by 'excessive force' you mean that I stopped a prophecy from detonating Soho and condemning London to a century of plague and bad musical theatre, then yes, I may have gone a touch overboard."

A couple of the vampires snorted, more in surprise than amusement. Blackthorn's face didn't move so much as flex, as if recalibrating its settings from "icy" to "absolute zero."

"Your restraint is legendary, Lupo," he said. "There is, however, a distinction between containment and... spectacle. You exposed a secret, centuries in the making, to the mortals. Some of whom, as you know, have camera phones."

Vincent bit back the urge to ask whether the Council still thought Polaroids were the height of technological menace. "With respect, Elder, if you'd allocated even a fraction of your resources to tracking prophecy-accelerants, rather than putting me on hold for six months, maybe we wouldn't be having this conversation?"

Blackthorn's eyebrow twitched—a seismic event, by his standards. "The resources of the Council are not subject to the whims of the disgraced," he pronounced, with the grandiosity of a man reading his own Wikipedia page aloud. "If you had followed due process—"

"Due process?" Mrs Barley interjected, voice crisp as

sheeted linen. "If I may, Elder, the applicant did, in fact, file two requests for ritual backup, one for tactical support, and three addenda via the Emergency Memoir channel, all of which were, to my knowledge, rerouted to the Penalty File."

There was a distinct, collective wince from the Council at "Emergency Memoir," a system introduced during the eighties by a particularly neurotic Elder who believed every disaster should be immediately immortalised in diary form. Mrs Barley, unbothered, began flipping through her notes ready to provide more evidence in support of Vincent.

Blackthorn ignored her with the professionalism of a man who'd spent centuries pretending the help didn't exist. "We are not here to debate the merits of your application. We are here because, thanks to your...initiative, the mortals are now aware of 'vampire activity' within Central London. We've spent years grooming their collective imagination to see vampires as a metaphor for tax avoidance, not a nightly hazard."

Ren coughed. "Technically, no one believed it until a cultist set himself on fire, ran out into the street, and started chanting in Latin. That part wasn't our fault."

The nearest vampire, an elegant relic in a silk dressing gown, eyed Ren like she was a beetle on his scone. "The conduct of your human associate is not under review," he said, making it sound like a deeply regrettable oversight. "Though one does wonder how you managed to accrue so many, given your past performance reviews."

Vincent shrugged. "I'm a people person."

Mrs Barley leaned sideways to murmur, "There's a note in the appendix. It says, 'avoid charm-related puns.'"

He grinned at her, which earned a look of maternal disgust. "It's only a war crime if you repeat it three times," he whispered.

Blackthorn's hand came down on the podium with a dry thud. "Enough. Lupo, you are hereby charged with the following: reckless endangerment of the masquerade, unauthorised contact with Council-sensitive artefacts, and gross failure to apply containment protocols." He paused, savouring the last as if it tasted of dark chocolate. "How do you plead?"

Vincent considered pleading "hungry," but opted for a diplomatic shrug. "Guilty, but with mitigating circumstances."

Ren raised a finger. "Mitigating circumstances being the literal end of the world?"

There was a titter from the shadows—one of the proxies, or maybe just an actual shadow with a sense of humour. The Council collectively stiffened, as if caught in an indecorous moment by a passing bishop.

Blackthorn sighed. "You're not entirely without value, Lupo, which is why the Council has agreed to... alternative sanctions."

Vincent steeled himself for a return to paperwork hell, or—worse—mandatory attendance at the quarterly banquets.

"Effective immediately," Blackthorn intoned, "you will be assigned to field observation of the Modernisers. Stakeouts. Surveillance. Babysitting the next generation until they learn to behave—or until you prove you can be trusted to operate among them without incident."

This provoked actual laughter from the marzipan effigy, which Vincent could have sworn gained a new wrinkle around the mouth.

"Babysitting," he echoed. "Is that what we're calling it now?"

Mrs Barley straightened her already ramrod posture. "Excuse me, Elder, but would you kindly clarify the terms of this assignment? There's been a noted lack of specificity in prior Council communiqués."

Blackthorn seemed to shrink, just a millimetre, as if pressed by the full weight of Mrs Barley's administrative prowess. "You will be responsible for monitoring all known Moderniser activity in your sector. Reports to be filed daily. Any deviation will result in immediate... dismissal."

He didn't specify what form "dismissal" might take. Vincent doubted it involved a generous severance package and a carriage clock.

Ren stared at Vincent, wide-eyed. "You're not going to make me wear a uniform, are you?"

"Only if you all want matching badges," he said, not quite joking.

The rest of the Council rose, or mimed rising, in a show of finality. Blackthorn gave one last glower, the kind that might have withered lesser men but only made Vincent itch to light a cigarette and blow smoke rings at the banners.

Dismissed, the trio made their way out. Behind them, the Council chamber returned to its natural state: an endless debate about etiquette, conducted by the undead for the benefit of absolutely no one.

In the corridor, Mrs Barley exhaled. "That went better than expected."

Vincent blinked. "You expected worse?"

She nodded. "Last time, they used the word 'exsanguination' six times before we got to the tea break. This was positively breezy."

Ren grinned. "So. Who are the Modernisers, exactly?"

Vincent considered lying, but only for a moment. "Vampires with a flair for social media. Last week one of them staged a flashmob at the British Library. The week before, someone tried to livestream a bloodletting ritual. Most of them are harmless, but a few... have ambition."

Ren's eyes lit up. "So, we're... supernatural mall cops."

Vincent groaned. "Don't let them catch you saying that. It'll end up on a T-shirt."

Mrs Barley was already halfway down the hall, muttering about the logistics of daily reporting and the utter lack of proper office supplies. Vincent hung back, letting Ren set the pace.

"Seriously," she said, after a few steps. "Why didn't you ask for the badges?"

He glanced sideways at her. "I think they'll make us wear something much, much worse."

And as they passed under the banners, their shadows stretched behind them—three shapes in lockstep, none of which quite matched the bodies they left behind.

There was a special category of room in London set aside for unpleasant tasks and even less pleasant conversations, and the office annex at the back of the Archives was the exemplar from which all others took their inspiration. The paint peeled in sheets from the cornices like burnt skin, the fluorescent lights hummed with the steady menace of a thousand agitated hornets, and the radiators functioned mainly as historical curiosities. A single desk and two battered chairs divided the space, though most of the floorspace was occupied by a siege rampart of filing cabinets, each bearing a hand-lettered label designed to induce existential despair.

Mrs Barley had commandeered the desk, and was at present arranging a set of manila folders with the devotion of a priestess preparing for sacrificial rites. She didn't so much as glance up as Vincent and Ren shuffled in, trailing the distinctive air of disciplinary action in their wake.

Vincent stared at the folders. "Is this where you tell us we've been reassigned to the vampire version of Ofsted?"

Mrs Barley gave him a look that could have stripped paint, had there been any left to strip. "Not Ofsted. More Ofwatch. Oversight, not improvement."

Ren edged a chair out with her boot and flopped into it, looking around with frank, undisguised curiosity. "Is that blood on the ceiling, or just the world's worst water damage?"

"Bit of both," Mrs Barley said, making a note in the ledger she'd produced from thin air. "The previous occupant believed in hands-on discipline."

Vincent massaged his temples. "Is there coffee?"

She slid a jar of freeze-dried horror in his direction, along with a chipped mug whose interior was the colour of ancient leather. He declined with a shake of the head. Ren, meanwhile, had helped herself and was now eyeing the folders like they might bite.

Mrs Barley cleared her throat. "Right. You are now the official observation unit for the Moderniser sub-cabal, North

Sector. Your primary contacts are detailed in these briefings." She flicked the folders open, one for each of them. "We have here: a blood-smoothie establishment operating out of a repurposed Costa, a retail operation specialising in occult-themed streetwear, and a network of content creators who appear to have trouble keeping their glamour up when live-streaming."

Ren whistled, leafing through the "blood-smoothie bar" dossier. "They really called it Hemogoblins?"

Mrs Barley's nostrils flared, but she did not dignify the question with a response. "You'll shadow their activities, document any breaches of the veil, and file nightly reports. The Council expects absolute compliance. Any deviation will result in disciplinary measures. And, given your previous form, the Council is watching you with special interest."

Vincent flicked through his own folder, scanning the faces. He recognised two: Cassian Roe, professional vampire influencer and part-time pyramid scheme architect; and Aurelia Voss, who had weaponised her Instagram to launch a "vampire wellness" empire, complete with branded teeth-whitening kits. There was a third face: Nyx Calder, a DJ whose main crime appeared to be running a semi-legal club night in a basement that hadn't seen daylight since the General Strike.

He closed the folder with a snap. "We really are babysitters."

"Stakeout officers," Mrs Barley corrected, though her heart wasn't in it.

Ren tapped her own folder, amusement in her voice. "At least it's fieldwork. Better than being stuck in this deathtrap."

On cue, the lights stuttered, and a chill crept up from beneath the floorboards. Vincent grunted, "Careful what you wish for," just as Zara Delacourt surfaced through the wooden slats, spectral form a few notches paler than usual, hair static-charged and eyes full of sarcasm.

She gave a two-fingered salute. "Reporting for the last ride of the deadbeat cavalry."

Ren startled, sloshing instant coffee onto the table. Zara leaned over her, reading the top folder upside-down. "Ah, Hemogoblins. Their O-negative blend tastes like rubber cement, but the staff are easy on the eyes. Did the Council at least spring for an expense account?"

Vincent set his folder down and addressed the ceiling. "If this is the afterlife, I want to speak to the manager."

Mrs Barley ignored the phantasm, opting instead to outline the next steps with the same brisk efficiency she reserved for housework and eldritch containment. "You'll begin with the Hemogoblins site. According to the last audit, there's been a spike in suspicious activity—youngbloods loitering after closing, unexplained energy surges, and a viral dance challenge that ends with participants blacking out and quoting Sumerian texts."

Zara grinned. "Not the worst Tuesday I've had."

Ren looked at Vincent, then at Zara. "So, what's our angle? Blend in, or just... lurk?"

"Blend," Vincent said, voice flat. "We're supposed to look like we belong."

"Which, in Vincent's case, means acting like an absentee headmaster who's given up on the curriculum," Zara said, earning a glare.

Mrs Barley clicked her pen for emphasis. "I must remind you all: We observe. We do not intervene. We document but do not engage. If a situation becomes unstable, you are to withdraw and notify me at once. The last thing we need is a repeat of what happened at the Orpheum, or worse, a livestream gone viral."

Ren, undeterred, started flicking through Zara's file. "You know all these people?"

"Most," Zara said. "Some from the before-times, some from the 'accidentally summoned to the wrong party' circuit. Voss used to crash my lectures. Cassian once tried to sell me a time-share in Romania. Nyx... we don't talk about Nyx."

Vincent hefted the folder under his arm, the universal gesture of "let's get this over with." He paused at the door. "If anyone needs me, I'll be at Hemogoblins, pretending to care about artisanal plasma and not putting any of this on TikTok."

Zara followed him, dematerialising as she went, while Ren hung back a moment, watching Mrs Barley stack the remaining folders with military precision.

"Is this going to be awful?" Ren asked.

Mrs Barley glanced up, surprise flickering across her features. "Statistically, yes. But I've seen you handle worse."

Ren nodded, and for the first time since entering the archive, looked almost reassured.

The instant the door shut, Mrs Barley opened a hidden compartment in the bottom drawer and withdrew a very old, very battered thermos. She poured herself a finger of what looked suspiciously like gin, and raised it in salute to the retreating chaos.

"To paperwork, and the ones foolish enough to believe it matters."

Vincent, meanwhile, was already striding out into the night, folder clamped tight and mind on the job. He muttered to himself as the cold air hit: "I already vanished once. How much harder can it be the second time?"

Behind him, the building hummed with ancient, unspeakable bureaucracy, gears turning in darkness, waiting for the next mess to be made.

TWO

If the purpose of surveillance was to remain inconspicuous, nobody had thought to mention it to the Council's fleet manager. Their van, a two-tonne diesel relic with the structural integrity of a well-used urinal, advertised its purpose only to those with a keen eye for body filler and suspiciously fresh number plates. It shuddered with each passing bus as if protesting the indignity of its assignment, and the passenger-side door had given up entirely, held shut by an elaborate system of bungee cords and what looked like a dog collar.

They were parked across the street from Hemogoblins, a Moderniser-run blood-smoothie bar whose shopfront bathed the pavement in a constant strobe of red-and-white LED. The interior was all clinical surfaces and designer stains; shelves stacked with gleaming vials labelled things like "Haemo-Boost" and "B Positive Bomb." Even the chalkboard outside—"Happy Hour, 18:00-20:00, bring a friend, get a free scone"—looked as if it had been written by someone with an Instagram sponsorship and a deep-seated grudge against lowercase.

Vincent had commandeered the passenger seat, though his sprawl suggested more of a Romanov in exile than any kind of operative. He balanced a pair of cheap binoculars on his lap, not because he needed them but because it annoyed Mrs Barley, who insisted on using her own set with the precision of a sniper. Ren was behind them, perched on a collapsible camp stool and hunched over a clipboard, highlighter uncapped and poised for action.

"Blood-orange detox shot," Vincent read off the menu board, squinting through the glass. "Should've stuck with O+ on tap. At least it's honest."

Ren made a noise halfway between a snort and a laugh, but didn't look up. "They have a loyalty programme. You get a commemorative enamel pin if you survive five visits."

"Modern vampires," Vincent mused. "All the hunger, none of the poetry."

"Some would say that's progress," Mrs Barley replied, her tone as flat as the van's rear near-side tyre. She had spread an oilcloth over her knees to catch stray biro ink, and was methodically working through a stack of triplicate forms, each bearing a hand-stamped warning: "COUNCIL USE ONLY—IMPROPER HANDLING MAY INCUR PENALTIES." Her thermos was perched on the dashboard, within easy reach but safely beyond the blast radius of Vincent's gesticulations.

Vincent risked a glance through his own binoculars, then set them down. "Is it just me, or are they mixing the blood with turmeric? Isn't that, like, a war crime?"

Ren didn't dignify it with a response. Her notes were colour-coded: yellow for suspected fangwork, red for confirmed vampiric influencers, purple for "miscellaneous sketchiness." She seemed genuinely invested, which Vincent found both touching and a little unnerving.

They lapsed into silence, the sort that collects in the corners of libraries and hospital waiting rooms, only more so because nobody wanted to admit they were bored. Every ten minutes, a teenager in shredded skinny jeans and a suspiciously vintage leather jacket would drift out of Hemogoblins, consult their phone, and wander off into the night. Sometimes they paired up, sometimes they argued about the best tube line for post-curfew parties, but not once did anyone explode, transform into a bat, or otherwise misbehave in a way the Council would consider actionable.

Eventually, Vincent got bored enough to start a fight.

He turned to Mrs Barley, who was now ticking boxes with the sort of grim efficiency one usually reserves for dental extractions. "Do you ever worry you're not living up to your full potential, Mrs B? I mean, all this time spent training, and now you're basically a traffic warden."

She did not look up. "I am perfectly content in my role, thank you."

Ren grinned without glancing up. "She has a spreadsheet for contentment. It updates hourly."

Vincent huffed. "What about you, Ren? Is this the exciting life of supernatural espionage you always dreamed of? Watching goth kids mainline carrot juice and trauma?"

Ren capped her highlighter with a flourish. "I don't know,

Vincent. I think I was hoping for a bit more 'sexy secret society with a dark academia aesthetic' and a bit less 'stakeout in a bin lorry.'"

He smirked. "You should see the dress code for Council banquets. Nothing says erotic like polyester capes and a sixteen-page non-disclosure."

The van rocked gently as Mrs Barley adjusted her seat, spine still ruler-straight. "If you two are quite finished, perhaps we could return to the assignment."

He waggled his eyebrows at her. "What, you're not even a little bit curious what's inside?"

"I know precisely what's inside," Mrs Barley said, and ticked another box with enough force to perforate all three sheets. "One hundred and fourteen litres of vegan-supplemented plasma, five unregistered Moderniser initiates, and, if I'm not mistaken, a small dog."

Ren looked up at this. "Dog?"

"Spaniel, possibly a rescue. They brought it in the back entrance at half seven."

Vincent looked at Ren. "You get used to it. She knows everything, stores it in a box, and never lets you have any unless you say please."

Mrs Barley made a note: "Subject Lupo, habitual exaggeration, possible attention-seeking." She didn't quite smile, but the corners of her mouth made a bid for freedom.

The awkwardness returned, now tinged with the slight irritation of people who know they'll be stuck together until at least midnight. Vincent fiddled with the radio, which offered only static and a single station playing Turkish rap. He drummed his fingers on the dash.

Then, without warning, the temperature in the van dropped four degrees. The air pressure shifted in a way that did things to Vincent's eardrums he didn't care to repeat. An anomalous fog billowed up from the footwell, and through it stepped Zara, intangible and glowing slightly at the edges, like a screensaver from the afterlife.

She took stock of the cramped quarters, then let out a low whistle. "I see the Council is really splashing out these days. Should've called in sick and haunted the multiplex."

Vincent recovered first. "There's no haunting the living, Zara. Rules are clear."

She rolled her eyes. "I'm not haunting, darling, I'm auditing. They said I could remote-assist from the beyond."

Ren gawked. "You... How long have you been here?"

Zara grinned, teeth dazzling, eyes a little too sharp. "Long enough to see you spell 'influencer' wrong on your grid."

Ren blushed, snapping the clipboard closed. "It's American spelling. Blame the algorithm."

Mrs Barley, to her credit, didn't blink. "You're interfering with Council protocol, Ms Delacourt."

"Am I? Or am I providing valuable cross-dimensional insight?" Zara perched her non-corporeal self on the armrest, then leaned over to peer at the blood bar through the window. "God, I used to date people like this. Bragged about their resting heart rate. No stamina at all."

Vincent snorted, unable to help himself. "At least they don't light up like a chandelier every time they enter a room."

Zara stuck her tongue out, but it flickered in and out like a gif. "Jealousy is an ugly look, Vincent."

He considered a retort, but was interrupted by a sudden

burst of movement outside. A group of three Modernisers—two in matching tracksuits, one in a cape made of what looked like tinfoil—posed in front of Hemogoblins, filming each other on a phone rigged with an LED ring. The display was part TikTok dance, part blood-drinking parody, and all mortifying.

Ren groaned. "Oh god, they're doing the 'Thirst Trap Challenge.' That's the one where you fake a haemorrhage, then chug beetroot juice. There were like ten hospital admissions last week."

Vincent eyed the performance with distaste. "The Council should be embarrassed by their outfits alone."

Mrs Barley logged the incident, her pen scratching like a deathwatch beetle. "Document but do not engage," she said. "If they start a flashmob, we're authorised to call in riot control."

"I could always scare them straight," Zara offered. "Literally. I have the means to induce mild cardiac events."

"No," said Mrs Barley, not even looking up. "We're on observation only."

Zara pouted, then shimmered sideways and poked Ren in the shoulder. "See you back at the flat later. You might want to give the living room a bit of clean."

Ren looked startled. "I just hadn't got round to it."

"I'm not keeping tabs, just y'know, everything in its place." Zara winked, then let her arm dematerialise through the dash for effect.

Vincent shook his head. "I swear, this city needs a better class of ghost."

Zara's image flickered, as if she was buffering. "Careful, or I'll take up residence in your liver."

"Too late," Vincent muttered. "Alcohol's got the lease."

Mrs Barley finally put down her pen. "We're here for another two hours. I suggest you make yourselves useful."

Zara floated up and out through the van roof, leaving a chill and the faint smell of ozone behind. Ren started scribbling again, clearly unsettled, and Mrs Barley resumed her paperwork. Vincent, for his part, simply watched the parade of nocturnal absurdity on the other side of the street, wondering at what point immortality had turned into the world's slowest and least satisfying reality show.

The night refused to move at anything faster than a crawl. For the first hour, Vincent managed to amuse himself by trying to identify the strains of music leaking from Hemogoblins' Bluetooth speakers. It was mostly EDM, punctuated by a kind of polyphonic wailing that made him nostalgic for the Gregorian chant ringtones of the early 2000s.

After the second hour, he was less entertained. His knees hurt from being wedged against the glove compartment, and his attempts to smoke out the window had resulted in a drift of ash that immediately boomeranged back into the van, peppering Ren's notes with the gentle insistence of volcanic fallout. She glared at him, but said nothing, a masterclass in silent suffering.

He squirmed, cracked his knuckles, and risked a glance at the dashboard clock. "Is it just me, or is time actually slowing down?"

Ren flipped a page, unamused. "Welcome to stakeout work.

It's all the thrill of watching grass grow, but with more risk of haemorrhoids."

He snorted. "I could murder a bottle of wine."

Mrs Barley, who hadn't taken her eyes off the bar for nearly thirty minutes, replied, "You could, but you won't. Council rules prohibit inebriation during active surveillance."

"I'm not surveilling, I'm observing," Vincent said, with the confidence of a man who believed wordplay was a legitimate legal defence.

"Semantics will not save you from Council discipline," Mrs Barley said, not unkindly, but with the finality of a librarian shushing a toddler. "Now hush, please."

Vincent slouched, which was difficult given the van's seat was engineered to keep the driver at maximum discomfort and alertness. He reached for the ancient radio, but Ren smacked his hand away.

"You try that Turkish rap station again, and I swear I'll file a noise complaint."

He grinned. "You're learning."

Ren's discipline was starting to erode. The neat script of her notes had become jagged, and she'd abandoned the colour-coded scheme somewhere around ten-thirty. Instead, she was doodling in the margins: fanged smiley faces, tiny impaled bats, a caricature of Vincent with his head replaced by a wine bottle.

He looked over her shoulder, squinting. "You've used three different shades of red tonight. Is there a vampire colour wheel I should know about?"

She capped the pen, not meeting his eye. "I like to keep my options open."

Outside, the blood bar's crowd thinned as midnight crept

closer, but the last remaining Modernisers seemed determined to wring every drop of drama from the evening. A pair of heavily-inked blondes staged a fake break-up on the steps, one throwing an artisanal smoothie in the other's face before storming off in tears. Vincent awarded style points for the arc of the liquid, and made a mental note to recruit them for future operatic distractions.

Ren's sigh was audible, as was her annoyance. "If we had a camera, we could just livestream this to the council and be done."

"That's exactly the problem," Vincent said. "They want to be watched. They're like exhibitionist cats, except instead of knocking stuff off shelves, they start cults and crash charity fun runs."

He noticed Mrs Barley had fallen oddly quiet. He checked to see if she was asleep, but her eyes were open, watching the Hemogoblins' interior like it was a tele-novella. Her fingers tapped an irregular tattoo against her thermos, and her paperwork lay untouched. For a moment, Vincent thought she'd finally run out of boxes to tick.

Ren caught his glance, shrugged. "She's doing the thing where she plays back every second of the last three hours in her head, looking for anomalies."

Vincent grunted. "She should bottle that and sell it as a sleep aid."

The minutes crawled, and the air in the van thickened with the stink of old upholstery and existential malaise. Outside, the final act of the night unfolded: three Modernisers, dressed in matching retro windbreakers, set up a tripod just beyond the bar's entrance. They arranged themselves in a human pyramid, one holding a smoothie aloft, the others howling at the moon.

Vincent watched, eyebrows climbing. "What fresh hell is this?"

Ren peered through the smudged window. "I told you, it's a thirst-trap thing. The latest trend is to stage an 'accidental' blood spill for maximum likes. If you time it with the midnight bell, your account gets boosted."

Vincent shuddered. "And I thought the old days were bad."

The pyramid collapsed, all three landing in a heap. The smoothie splattered everywhere, then rolled into the gutter, forgotten. The girls screeched, took selfies with the mess, and vanished into the night.

Vincent glanced back at Mrs Barley. "You want to note that down, or just score them on creativity?"

She didn't blink. "Documented. The only anomaly is the lack of real blood. The Council will be... relieved."

He almost felt sorry for her.

The rest of the shift ticked by with the slow agony of a time dilation experiment. The bar closed, its neon signage winking off with a hiss, and the surrounding street slipped back into its usual fug of bin bags and drizzle. Only then did Mrs Barley speak again.

"Time to pack up. Please observe Council sign-off protocol."

Vincent rolled his eyes. "Is there a form for that, or can we just pinkie-swear?"

Mrs Barley ignored the jibe, producing a laminated checklist from her satchel. Ren slumped in her seat, closing her notebook with the resigned thump of a failed exam.

As Vincent clambered out of the van, his knees popping like

bubble wrap, he stretched and eyed the street. Not a single supernatural disturbance, no prophecies on fire, just a trio of hungover Modernisers and a spilled smoothie slowly congealing in the gutter.

He looked back at the van, at Ren and Mrs Barley, and the mountain of forms they'd generated over one of the most pointless nights of his unlife.

"Told you," he said to Ren, feeling both vindicated and vaguely suicidal. "Vampire babysitting."

She pulled her beanie low over her eyes. "You're the worst supervisor I've ever had."

Mrs Barley locked the doors and stood, stretching her back like a drill sergeant at parade rest. "Let's all remember to submit our individual reports before sunrise," she said, "and do try to avoid unnecessary embellishment."

Vincent gave her a mock salute. "Aye, aye, Council Mum."

She did not dignify that with a response.

They started off down the pavement, the three of them in a jagged line, leaving the van to its fate under a flickering streetlamp. Hemogoblins would open again tomorrow, and the same charade would play out, and maybe, if the Council was lucky, they'd catch someone with a genuinely illegal smoothie.

Vincent didn't look forward to it. He had a sudden, inexplicable craving for something real: red wine, a proper fight, or a reason to care about any of it.

Instead, he fell in step with Ren and Mrs Barley, the paperwork already multiplying in his mind. They made their way home through the night, one foot after the other, with the unhurried resignation of people who knew their best years were in the rear-view mirror.

At the corner, Ren asked, "Do you think the Modernisers know we're watching?"

Vincent shrugged. "They're narcissists. Of course they do."

Mrs Barley clicked her pen, eyes on the horizon. "Good. Maybe they'll behave for once."

The three of them vanished into the drizzle, and behind them, the city buzzed on, indifferent and unchanging, waiting for the next shift to begin.

THREE

It had taken three nights, almost an entire tank of diesel, and half a carton of Marlboros for Vincent to decide he hated Hemogoblins even more than he'd hated his own turning. The Moderniser blood bar had, by some act of architectural perversion, converted what used to be a tasteful Georgian printworks into a cross between an abattoir and a late-stage Berlin techno club. Even at a hundred yards, the LED frontage spat enough photonic venom to leave after-images on the insides of his eyelids, and the sub-bass pounded through the van's chassis with the persistence of a bailiff at a student flat.

He slouched in the passenger seat, knees wedged against the battered glove box, arms folded, and eyes closed as if it might blunt the pain. The speakers inside the bar pulsed so hard he could feel the fillings in his teeth attempting to dance out of his gums. "It's like a migraine," he said, not for the first time, "but with a soundtrack."

From the rear bench, Ren was all business: legs pretzeled on the van's threadbare upholstery, notebook propped against a clipboard so splattered with highlighter it looked like it had been used for vivisection. She had four pens clipped to her beanie, each denoting a different Council status, and was halfway through a detailed timeline of the night's Moderniser ingress and egress.

She glanced up at Vincent's pained expression and snorted. "Don't act like you don't love it. Isn't this what you lot dreamt about in the crypts? Blood on tap, open till sunrise, every night's a party?"

He cracked one eye open and levelled a look at her. "We also dreamt about regular bin collection and running water, but nobody ever called that progress."

In the driver's seat, Mrs Barley maintained a posture of such impeccable verticality that Vincent was certain she'd had a titanium rod inserted at birth. She wore her uniform—charcoal suit, white gloves, silver hair in an unbudgeable bun—as if this was a UN peacekeeping mission rather than a tour of night-shift purgatory. Her binoculars were trained on Hemogoblins' main entrance, hands perfectly still save for the occasional, surgical adjustment.

She cleared her throat without lowering the glasses. "Observation requires discipline, Mr Lupo. You might consider setting an example."

Vincent resisted the urge to salute. "I'd be more disciplined if I didn't have to listen to the awful music."

Ren scribbled a note, then addressed Mrs Barley. "If I went inside, just for a look, I could record what they're saying to customers. Council wants specifics, not just a head count."

"Negative," Mrs Barley replied, tapping a form as if the ink alone could bludgeon Ren into compliance. "Per protocol, observers must maintain a minimum thirty-metre distance. If you enter, you risk contaminating the event profile."

Vincent rolled his eyes, fishing a battered hip flask from his coat pocket. "Council logic: better to risk missing an apocalypse than smudge the paperwork."

Ren twisted round, facing him. "You have zero curiosity. Seriously, don't you want to know what they're actually doing in there?"

"I know exactly what they're doing," Vincent said, and took a swig. "Nothing good has ever happened at a rave called 'Bleed the Beat.'"

He gestured out the windscreen, where a queue of punters snaked round the block, half in costume, half in what Vincent privately considered "mid-tier cosplay for the easily bored." Some of them wore white paper surgeon masks with cut-out fangs, others sported t-shirts that read "NO BLOOD FOR OIL" or "#THIRSTTRAP." Every so often, one of the Modernisers would emerge from the bar, face streaked with deliberately-smeared lipstick, and conduct a lap of the pavement, arms raised as if greeting the adulation of a crowd that was, in fact, mostly there for the free drink tokens.

The van's dashboard was an archaeological record of their last three stakeouts: petrified takeaway wrappers (Ren, mostly), a spread of A4 briefing sheets (Mrs Barley), and at least two empty bottles of Malbec (Vincent, definitely). An old radio, patched into the cigarette lighter with a coil of wires that threatened to short out at any moment, played an endless loop of traffic updates interspersed, tonight, with Italian football commentary.

Ren glanced at her phone, scrolled the Modernisers' hashtag, and muttered, "They're live-streaming again. Want to see?"

Mrs Barley bristled. "Electronic communication within the observation perimeter is a Class Four risk."

"Only if you're worried about malware," Ren replied, rolling her eyes. "And the Council issued me this phone. They're probably monitoring me more than the Modernisers, anyway."

Vincent made a vague gesture that might have been "go ahead" or "burn the phone," depending on the angle. Ren thumbed up the stream and set the phone on the dash for all to see.

The camera shuddered, panned through strobes and writhing bodies, then settled on the stage. A DJ, in full dental surgeon drag, was mixing tracks behind a pulpit made from what looked like repurposed MRI equipment. On either side, Moderniser acolytes danced with the fervour of people who didn't have to worry about electrolyte depletion or the long-term effects of ketamine.

Over the PA, a woman's voice—amplified, autotuned, but unmistakably Aurelia Voss—addressed the crowd.

"Tonight," she said, "we rewrite history. We shed the chains of secrecy. We show the world what true appetite means!"

The crowd howled approval. The comment feed on Ren's phone scrolled so fast it became a blur of hearts, fangs, and eggplant emojis.

Vincent rolled his head back, thumping it gently against the van window. "For this I went to Oxford," he said, "twice."

Mrs Barley made another note in her ledger, unamused.

"Content remains within established parameters. They have not yet deviated from approved rituals."

"Except the part where they announce it to a hundred thousand followers," Ren said.

"That is not the anomaly," Mrs Barley replied. "The anomaly is that no one has attempted to monetise it yet."

Ren opened her mouth to retort, but was interrupted by a sudden atmospheric drop in the van's temperature, the kind that would make a polar bear reach for a jumper. A swirl of fog condensed through the dashboard vents and resolved, with theatrical flair, into Zara—still spectral, still overdressed, and still very much a pain in Vincent's existential rear.

She hovered above the dashboard like the world's most sarcastic sat-nav, glancing from Vincent to Mrs Barley to Ren and back again.

"God, you're still in here?" she asked, voice echoing in that weird, double-layered way ghosts favoured. "If I had a body, I'd already be inside dancing."

Vincent started, sloshing a little from his flask onto his trousers. "Zara. You're supposed to be auditing. Not haunting."

"I am auditing," she said. "From a safe distance. Besides, it's standing room only in there, and I'd hate to catch a virtual STD."

Mrs Barley looked as if she'd bitten down on a lemon. "Can you please not materialise through Council property? It voids the warranty."

Zara grinned. "Tell that to the last three drivers who tried to park this thing on double yellows. They're still reliving the experience in their sleep."

Ren, delighted, angled her phone towards Zara. "You want a peek? They're doing the Thirst Trap Challenge again."

Zara watched, face twisting in amusement and a little nostalgia. "Oh, I know this one. Wait, pause it—there. See the DJ's setlist?"

Ren squinted, then pinched to zoom. "Looks like... a standard playlist? A lot of nineties pop remixed with weird Gregorian chanting."

"Not the titles," Zara said, finger phased through the phone. "The lyrics. That's... familiar."

Vincent took the phone and looked at the screen. The lyrics, scrolling in time with the beat, were a mashup of Latin phrases, New Age platitudes, and—every so often—a line that gave him a sharp, unpleasant twinge of recognition.

Ren noticed his reaction. "What is it?"

He handed the phone to Mrs Barley, who scanned the display with professional detachment. Then, very slowly, she put the phone down.

"It's a derivation," she said, "of Carmine's prophecy. Someone's woven the text into a rave anthem."

Zara shrugged. "Art imitates unlife."

Ren blinked, suddenly serious. "Does that mean—we didn't destroy the prophecy? Or someone just messing with us?"

"Hard to say," Vincent replied, rubbing his temples. "Either way, it's not going to end in a conga line."

As they watched, the crowd inside Hemogoblins swelled to fever pitch. The beat went double-time, and the LEDs strobed so rapidly that Ren had to look away. On screen, the Modernisers started moving in synchrony, arms raised, faces distorted by the low-light and cheap camera filters.

Vincent felt a slow, cold dread creep into his gut. He'd seen this kind of thing before: the moment a party crossed from "debauchery" into "mass psychosis." It always ended in one of two ways, and both required professional clean-up.

Zara let out a low, appreciative whistle. "That's not choreography. That's a summoning."

Mrs Barley closed her notebook with a snap. "The Council will need to see this."

Vincent stared at the phone, where the lyrics now scrolled in all caps: "FEED THE FUTURE. BLEED THE PAST. HISTORY IS WRITTEN IN BLOOD."

He put the phone down and said, mostly to himself, "And they say I'm the dramatic one."

They sat in silence, listening to the music grow louder, faster, more distorted. Somewhere across the street, a window shattered in perfect sync with the bassline.

"Should we... intervene?" Ren asked, voice very small.

Mrs Barley considered, then shook her head. "Not yet. Observation only."

Vincent poured the last of his flask onto the footwell and watched as the crowd on screen began to blur, their outlines twisting and interlocking until it looked less like a party and more like a feeding frenzy.

"Observation only," he repeated. But he didn't believe it for a second.

Hemogoblins, up close, stank of antiseptic, body spray, and the sweetish tinge of synthetic plasma. The bouncers on the door looked like they'd been drafted from the Olympic shot-put circuit, but inside, the only real security was a single line of polished brass and a "No Feral Behaviour" sign that nobody had ever read, let alone enforced.

Ren led the way, Vincent at her heels, and Mrs Barley bringing up the rear with the brisk efficiency of a funeral director. The music was, if possible, even louder in person, a wall of noise that pressed against the inside of Vincent's skull until his thoughts oozed out in short, clipped fragments.

He scanned the crowd, trying to get a read on the Moderniser population. It was a sea of pale faces, sequinned jackets, and aggressively unremarkable haircuts, all writhing in sync as if they shared a single, glitchy nervous system. The DJ—now standing on the stage—was still in surgeon drag, face a white mask with plastic blood spatters, but he didn't seem to be doing much. The mixing board was on autopilot, and his hands trembled at his sides, fingers spasming like the legs of an upturned insect.

Vincent leaned toward Ren, lips brushing her ear. "You getting anything useful?"

She shook her head, eyes wide. "It's all off. Everyone's too coordinated."

He watched as the crowd moved, each ripple of the bassline triggering a response that spread like a sympathetic convulsion from wall to wall. No one blinked. No one laughed, or checked their phones, or did any of the usual things young people did in a bar.

"Is it a trance?" Ren asked, shouting above the din.

"Not one I've seen," Vincent replied. He risked a glance at the mirrored wall behind the bar and immediately wished he hadn't: a hundred and fifty faces, each slightly out of sync with its owner, all staring back at him.

He nudged Ren, and together they pushed through the dancers. Mrs Barley followed, umbrella tucked under her arm like a katana, face set in grim determination.

They made it as far as the raised platform at the rear when the music cut mid-beat, leaving a vacuum so total it made Vincent's ears ring. For a split second, the entire room was frozen. Then the screens above the DJ booth flickered to life, and a line of text scrolled across, in font so large even the barflies could read it:

BLOOD IS MEMORY. BLOOD IS FUTURE. BLEED THE PAST.

The words repeated, strobing in sync with a new, weirder backing track: a layered chant that sounded like it had been run through an industrial blender. The crowd began to howl in unison, low and animal, and then the Modernisers started to change.

It was subtle at first—an elongation of the canines, a red tinge to the eyes, a flattening of affect. But as the chant reached its first crescendo, the changes accelerated. Glamours failed, and the influencers on the floor lost their carefully curated normalcy. Now they looked like what they actually were: half-starved youngbloods who had never learned how to play it cool.

A panic began to ripple, slowly at first, then with growing urgency as the more fragile humans realised something was off.

Phones came out, flashlights activated, and every corner of the club was instantly under a million-lumen gaze.

Vincent saw Zara appear at the edge of the stage, her ghostly form flickering with the ambient electromagnetic noise. She mouthed something at him—could've been "get down," could've been "run"—but before he could react, the first Moderniser leapt onto the bar, dropped a pint glass, and let out a scream that was pure hunger.

The crowd collapsed into chaos. Some tried to run, others froze, and a handful started filming, as if the end of the world might earn them a blue tick. On the main screens, the prophecy had switched to all caps:

HISTORY IS WRITTEN IN BLOOD.

Aurelia Voss, leading the chant from atop a podium, was fully transformed now. Her face was a mask of predatory glee, fangs bared, eyes alight with a kind of demonic charisma. She addressed the room as if delivering a TED talk on the benefits of mass hysteria.

"Tonight," she declared, "we break the narrative. No more hiding. No more shame. We are the new immortals!"

It was, Vincent thought, exactly the sort of thing Carmine would have arranged, if he had a taste for performance art.

Ren had her phone out, recording even as the club dissolved around them. Mrs Barley tried to drag her toward the exit, but Ren resisted, insisting she needed "hard evidence."

"You'll get hard evidence if you don't move," Mrs Barley hissed, and yanked her by the hood.

Vincent stayed a moment longer, gauging the flow of bodies. He spotted three Modernisers converging on the nearest group of panicking humans, all fang and claw and nightclub aggression. Without thinking, he stepped between them and the civilians.

"Not tonight," he said, and caught the first one by the neck. It was a kid, really, no older than Ren. He flailed, shrieked, then collapsed as Vincent squeezed just enough to cut the blood flow.

The next two were faster, but Vincent had centuries of experience and an unfortunate willingness to use it. He slammed one into a support column and the other into the mirrored wall, which shattered in a shower of safety glass.

Behind him, someone started screaming. He turned to see Mrs Barley getting busy with her umbrella, wielding it with the precision of a fencing master. Each jab landed with a percussive thud, and within seconds she had dispatched two more Modernisers and was advancing on a third.

Ren, still filming, yelled, "Vincent! The feed—look at the feed!"

He glanced at her phone, and saw that every single livestream was now showing the prophecy, superimposed in red over the writhing, blood-soaked dancefloor. The text flickered, then resolved into a face: Carmine's, rendered in pixelated monochrome, mouthing the words in perfect sync with the chant.

Vincent swore. "It's Carmine. He's hijacked the broadcast."

Ren looked up at him, terrified but also impressed. "Can he do that?"

"If you know Carmine, it's weirder that he hasn't done it sooner."

The chanting reached a final, brutal crescendo, and then all at once, the Modernisers dropped to the floor like marionettes with their strings cut. For a heartbeat, nobody moved. Then, with a collective groan, the survivors staggered to their feet, blinking and dazed.

Aurelia Voss, back on her feet, staggered to the front of the stage. Her face was smeared with blood—hers, or someone else's, it was hard to say. She pointed directly at the camera, and in a voice hoarse but unbroken, declared:

"This is our future. Watch it burn."

The music cut, and the screens went dark.

A long silence followed, broken only by the drip of fake blood from the ceiling fixtures.

Vincent found Mrs Barley, who was wiping her umbrella on the skirt of a toppled influencer. She looked at him with faint approval. "You did well."

"I broke a lot of furniture."

"It was a calculated risk."

He nodded, then turned to Ren, who was still streaming, hands shaking. "You okay?"

She nodded, lips white. "Did you see what was happening? With the face? That was—"

"Carmine," Vincent finished. "He's back, and he's escalating."

They made their way to the door, stepping over piles of unconscious Modernisers and the occasional puddle of leaking plasma. Outside, the queue had mostly scattered, but a handful of loyal fans still clustered under the awning, filming the aftermath.

"How do I look?" Vincent asked as they crossed the threshold back on to the street.

Mrs Barley looked him up and down. "No fangs, no glowing eyes, just a battered, hungover man in a borrowed coat."

"Possibly the nicest thing you've ever said to me. Thank you."

Behind them, the club's fire alarms kicked in, and a wash of red lights painted the street. Sirens wailed in the distance, though it was impossible to tell if they were for this disaster or the half-dozen others happening in Soho on a Saturday night.

They regrouped at the van, breathless and vibrating with adrenaline. Ren checked her phone, and saw that the hashtag #BleedTheFuture was already trending, alongside #Zombie-Rave and #VampireCult. Clips from inside Hemogoblins were being re-broadcast around the globe, each more doctored and deranged than the last.

Vincent slumped in the passenger seat, head in his hands. "It's out. The whole thing is out."

Mrs Barley climbed behind the wheel, umbrella laid across her lap like a baton of office. "The Council will be furious."

Ren, still pale, managed a laugh. "Maybe they'll send someone to actually help next time."

"Unlikely," Mrs Barley replied. "But we'll survive."

Vincent checked his hands, flexing his fingers. "For now."

They sat in silence, letting the music and chaos fade behind them. After a while, Ren said, "So what happens now?"

Vincent looked at her, and for once, didn't have a sarcastic answer. "We watch. We wait. And we hope Carmine hasn't got a part two."

Mrs Barley started the van, and with a shudder, they pulled

away from the curb. As they rounded the corner, Zara phased in through the window, perched herself on the dash, and said, "I give it twenty-four hours before someone tries this at home."

Ren groaned, but didn't disagree.

Vincent watched the rear-view mirror, half-expecting the club to erupt in flames, but it remained stubbornly intact, neon sign flickering in the drizzle.

FOUR

If the Court of Pale Affairs was an architectural warning, the Council's disciplinary suite was its nuclear option. Buried four levels below street, the chamber combined the gloom of a mass grave with the acoustics of a swimming pool. Some creative type had tried to disguise the effect with iron wall sconces and pleather benches, but the result merely suggested an after-hours tribunal at a failing crematorium. Rows of seats, uncomfortably tiered and upholstered in something that looked like sharkskin, faced a central well where the condemned were expected to perform their contrition.

Tonight, the condemned were three, and only one of them had bothered to iron her shirt.

Mrs Barley took her place in the pit, hair perfectly coiled, tablet clutched in white-gloved hands like an ecclesiastical arte-fact. Ren hovered at her right, looking deeply unimpressed with the entire pageant, her jumper sleeve picked to shreds at the cuff. Vincent, naturally, had eschewed the row of provided chairs, and instead draped himself over a structural column, arms folded, expression set to "show me the deathtrap."

At the summit of the room, Elder Mortimer Blackthorn presided from a throne so ostentatious it would have embarrassed the Habsburgs. He wore his Order's robes like a skin condition, every fold calculated to emphasise a general air of pestilential disapproval. His fingers, long as spider legs, drummed the armrest in a rhythm designed to unsettle.

"Proceed, Mrs Barley," he intoned, as if delivering the final word at a particularly adversarial funeral.

She nodded and, without preamble, began her presentation. The screen behind her flickered to life, throwing up a collage of digital evidence: timestamped screenshots, glitched out images of Hemogoblins' dance floor, overlays of chat logs and comment feeds that painted a less-than-rosy picture of vampire discretion.

"Council, I submit for the record: at 22:19, the first in a series of Moderniser livestreams went public, attracting over ninety thousand concurrent viewers in the first ten minutes. Within five minutes, the Moderniser lead—Aurelia Voss—had orchestrated a public declaration of unseelie alignment. The event escalated at 22:33, when the crowd entered collective trance, and at 22:41, all physical and digital glamours failed. Multiple human witnesses present. At least four news agencies and seventeen social influencers have since reposted the footage. The full, uncensored videos are currently available in eighty-three distinct locations, including Reddit, TikTok, and, inexplicably, the website of a Sunderland fishmonger."

Blackthorn did not blink. "And the prophecy elements?"

Mrs Barley swiped forward. A slide appeared: blurry stills of the stage, DJ mid-collapse, arms thrown wide like a martyr in a budget horror film. In one, the scrolling lyrics—blood-red and frantic—were visible behind his head.

"Council will note the use of 'bleed the past' and 'history is written in blood' in all chanted material. The suspect Carmine's portrait appears as an avatar on multiple bootlegged streams, further amplifying the message."

There was a ripple of bored irritation from the higher benches. The younger vampires whispered among themselves, stifling laughter behind lacquered hands. A couple of the proxies—their flesh somewhere between playdough and candle-wax—looked at each other as if trying to work out what a DJ was.

Vincent could not help himself. "I told you. The DJ went full prophecy remix. Maybe next time the Council can just put the threat on a branded tote bag."

Blackthorn's face creaked a fraction, the barest hint of a smile, but he pressed on. "Let the record show: accused party displays continued lack of decorum. Ren, your statement?"

Ren, caught in mid-pick, gave an aggressive shrug. "Everything she said. Only it was worse in person. No one was faking it. The Modernisers wanted to be seen. Even the humans weren't scared until the very end—they just thought it was viral marketing for a horror film. There's nothing to clean up. Everybody already believes it."

One of the other elders, a withered woman whose entire skull was visible through her skin, leaned forward. "And what of the Council's own protocols? Did you file your report according to Section B, Subsection Twelve?"

Mrs Barley replied before Ren could start on the creative swearing. "Report filed within one hour, including full digital and physical logs, and triple authentication by myself, Ms Delacourt, and Mr Lupo. I appended the last seven Council directives concerning Moderniser propaganda. The Council appears to have ignored all of them."

There was a shuffling of papers and a long pause, broken only by the click of Blackthorn's fingernails on varnished oak. "So. You recommend what, exactly?"

Mrs Barley straightened her lapels, even though they had never been crooked. "Immediate escalation. The Modernisers are no longer attempting to keep the Veil. Their next action will be more overt, possibly violent. We require authority to engage directly, or at minimum, enhanced tactical support."

Another elder spoke, this one shaped like a starved penguin and possessing all the warmth. "Or perhaps your group could have contained it before it became public spectacle. Did you not have physical presence on site for three consecutive nights?"

Vincent bristled. "We did. We're talking of a crowd of over one hundred and zero backup. Unless you count a poltergeist and an umbrella."

Blackthorn raised a hand for silence. "Thank you, Mr Lupo, for reminding us of your team's... improvisational skillset."

He addressed the room at large. "It is the Council's view that the Moderniser sub-cabal's actions, while regrettable, constitute a calculated glamour malfunction, not a true breach. Furthermore, the so-called prophecy elements are easily ascribed to internet meme culture and the postmodern tendency toward self-parody. In short: no real harm done."

Mrs Barley's jaw muscles flickered, but she stayed silent.

"However," Blackthorn continued, "the team's failure to contain the initial incident has caused considerable reputational damage. Effective immediately, your surveillance duties are doubled. You will monitor all Moderniser activity in the Northern and Central sectors, and you will do so under direct Council oversight."

Ren glared. "So, we get to be the viral police. Again."

Blackthorn ignored her. "Should you fail to prevent further public embarrassment, the consequences will be... non-administrative."

Vincent muttered, "So, like, a sternly worded execution?"

The Council did not dignify it with a response.

"Any questions?" Blackthorn asked, though his tone implied it would be best if there weren't.

Mrs Barley inclined her head. "No, Elder. We accept the verdict."

Ren snorted, but nodded.

Vincent gave a salute so sarcastic it was practically a threat.

The session ended not with a bang, but with a shuffling of feet and a low-grade psychic malaise that left the entire chamber feeling two degrees colder.

As they filed out, Mrs Barley lingered a moment at the base of the stairs, her expression fixed but her hands trembling, very slightly, as she closed her tablet. Ren caught up, breath still shallow from contained rage.

"They're never going to believe us," she said, "even when it bites them in the arse."

Vincent joined, pushing off from his column. "They don't have to believe. They just have to not get blamed."

Mrs Barley's lips compressed to a line. "You are both correct."

Ren stopped at the exit, glancing over her shoulder at the Council's dais. "So, what now?"

"We watch," Mrs Barley said, voice low but steady. "We wait. And we do our jobs until the end of the world."

Vincent gave a thin smile. "And if we're lucky, we live long enough to see them clean up their own mess."

They left the mausoleum behind, the echo of the Council's judgment following them up the stairs and into the perpetual dark of the city above.

Zara's flat, which was now Ren's flat, was what estate agents called "charmingly lived-in" and what anyone with eyes called "a hoarder's mausoleum with character." It occupied the top floor of a terraced Victorian that had once been a single-family home, then a squat, then a patchwork of bedsits. Every inch of wall was obscured by shelves, whiteboards, and the kind of framed diploma that only seemed to multiply after death. In the middle of it all, a constellation of mismatched seating jostled for space with piles of takeaway cartons, a collapsed air mattress, and a surveillance array that looked one re-wire away from summoning extra-terrestrials.

Ren paced between the stacks, arms folded tight, body language set to "pre-explosion." She rattled off complaints with the clipped delivery of someone who'd rehearsed every line.

"Council's not just blind, they're actively malicious," she said, kicking aside a heap of loose cables. "It's like they want the prophecy to go off. Or maybe they think if they ignore it long enough, it'll fix itself."

Vincent, star-shaped across the sofa, swirled a glass of red and watched the wine leave reluctant arcs against the chipped rim. "The Council's had centuries of practice in the art of making things someone else's problem," he said. "It's basically their founding principle."

He raised the glass in a toast to no one, then drank as if aiming to anaesthetise his entire nervous system.

At the tiny kitchen table, Mrs Barley was hunched over her laptop, the glow throwing deep-set shadows across her face. She typed with the measured calm of a professional pianist, but every so often her hands trembled, and she had to steady them with a breath. Next to her, a neat stack of completed reports was weighted down by a jar of pickled onions. A full dossier's worth of evidence that, if she was honest, nobody was ever going to read.

A fizz of ozone, and Zara herself flickered into being, emerging through a standing lamp and casting a polychrome halo across the far wall. She inspected her own spectral palm, made a sound somewhere between a snort and a purr, and drifted through the living room like a bored weather balloon.

"Would you all relax?" she said, weaving around the TV. "You've gone full Hamlet and it's not even midnight. The livestreams are out. Damage done."

She glitched slightly as she passed through the coffee table, sending a minor flurry of Worcester sauce crisps into the air. "Honestly," she said, "you can't glamour away TikTok. Not even with a Council full of crypt keepers."

Ren stopped pacing just long enough to scowl. "So that's it? We just watch them meme themselves into the apocalypse?"

Zara shrugged, a ripple of fog passing through her shoulders. "That, or you start your own meme. Win the narrative. It's all public perception now, darling. Existence is branding."

Vincent snorted. "The first vampire war fought entirely with influencer campaigns. Carmine would be so proud."

Mrs Barley's typing halted. She sat there for a moment, hands clasped as if in prayer, then looked up at the group. Her face was tired, but her eyes were sharp. "This isn't containment. It's triage. The Council doesn't care who gets caught in the fire as long as the curtain stays closed."

Ren dropped onto a battered armchair, its stuffing visible through the armrest. "Then why are we doing this? What's the point of surveillance if the only rule is 'don't get caught?'"

Mrs Barley smiled, but there was no joy in it. "Because if we stop, there's nothing left between them and open warfare."

The room fell into a silence, punctuated only by the hum of the fridge and Zara's gentle oscillation near the bay window.

Vincent emptied his glass, then held the bottle up to the light. "We're running low," he said, voice flat. "Council won't reimburse us for morale supplies, either."

Zara slithered along the windowsill, casting prismatic bands onto the wall. "I could always haunt the off licence," she offered. "Spectral theft is low-risk, high reward."

Ren, finally spent, pulled her knees to her chest and fixed Vincent with a look. "If the Council won't stop Carmine, who will?"

He didn't answer. Instead, he poured a measured finger of

wine, set the bottle down, and stared into the glass like it contained the secret to not caring.

Mrs Barley began typing again, slower now. "I'll keep filing. I doubt it matters, but it's better than nothing."

Zara perched, for a moment, on the arm of the sofa, before dissolving into the next room. "The world's ending, but you're all so proper about it," she said, her voice echoing off the kitchen tiles. "Makes a ghost proud."

They sat with their tasks: Ren sulking, Mrs Barley recording, Vincent cultivating an air of chemical serenity. Outside, the city vibrated with traffic, a thousand parties, and at least one viral prophecy. Inside, they waited for the next disaster, or maybe for the Council to find a new scapegoat. Until then, they shared the bottle, the silence, and the certainty that whatever happened next, nobody was coming to rescue them.

And above it all, the prophecy ticked on, scribed in blood and data packets, while three almost-strangers watched history repeat itself from a living room in North London.

FIVE

Ren woke as if someone had poured cold bleach down her spine, the world resolving into focus with the kind of clarity that suggested something was broken. For a moment, she did not know where she was—only that she was sweating, heart going at war-drum pace, and that her left arm was on fire.

She sat up too fast. The bed's steel frame bit her in the thigh, and the air around her seemed to shimmer in double vision. The room was, for lack of a better word, haunted: every surface in Zara's flat heaved with the detritus of old research printouts, laundry, and the unnameable silt of months spent living on emergency rations and adrenaline. A faint strobe blinked in the street outside, lending everything the unreality of a crime scene on pause.

Ren clamped her good hand over her nose, which had started leaking again—and just like before, the blood was black, and left a shadow on the pillow that stank of iron filings and burnt toast. She tried to reach for a tissue, but her left arm refused to cooperate.

It took her a second to register the reason: the Editor's Mark, which had lived mostly dormant on her forearm since the Orpheum Theatre collapsed, was now pulsing in a blue-green that made her skin look like the dial of a cheap digital watch. The Mark had grown, she realised, now stretching from wrist to elbow in a network of sigils that looked for all the world like a map of the Northern Line, if the Northern Line had been planned by a sociopath with a fondness for Celtic knotwork. The glow threw moving shadows across the stacks of takeaway cartons and illuminated every fingerprint on the mug beside the sofa.

She swore, softly, then a little louder for good measure. Her phone had vibrated itself off the coffee table, landing wedged between two paperbacks of critical theory and what looked suspiciously like a vintage porn magazine. She fished it out, wiping her hand on the back of her sweatpants, and checked the time: 03:11. Of course it was.

She didn't need to check to know she'd been dreaming, because the taste of copper and ink was still fresh on her tongue, and her thoughts were full of stories that didn't belong to her. In the dream she'd been walking through a bone-dry field, watching a girl with her own face pour salt into the soil, spelling out words that vanished when you looked straight at them. Behind her, the world had burned blue and white, and Vincent was there, but his face kept glitching out, replaced by a flickering silhouette that made her want to cry.

She let her head fall back onto the sofa with a thud. A

feather of panic lingered at the edge of her vision, like the after-image of a flash bulb. "Fuck you," she muttered, to the Mark or the prophecy or both.

Something soft and papery floated down onto her knee. She flinched, because it was nowhere near her own stack of notes, and it hadn't been there before.

It was a scrap of paper, torn unevenly at the top, like a ransom note in a film. The writing on it was not hers, nor Zara's, nor anyone's she recognised, but it slashed across the page in confident black:

The girl will fall in line, or she will fall apart.

Ren stared at it, then at her arm, then at the note again. The Mark's glow had intensified, as if in smug self-congratulation.

"Oh, do fuck off," she said, but the paper just lay there, radiating threat.

Vincent appeared at the bedroom doorway, a mug of blood-coffee in one hand and an expression of calculated nonchalance on his face. He was barefoot, wearing only a T-shirt and whatever he'd salvaged from the laundry pile, but even half-asleep he moved with the awkward grace of someone who'd spent centuries forgetting how to look relaxed.

He clocked the scene instantly: Ren on the bed, nose bleeding black onto the pillow, arm glowing, and a mystery note on her knee.

"Sleep well?" he asked, voice light as a spent match.

She grunted, and for a moment the only sound was the building's ancient pipes grumbling in sympathy.

Vincent crossed to the bed, set down the mug with a care that suggested it was the last clean one in the flat, and then hovered. "That looks... lively," he said, nodding at her arm.

Ren wiped her nose, which was now trickling a kind of viscous, tarry blue. "You ever dream in third-person omniscient?" she asked, words pinched through gritted teeth.

He made a face. "Don't sleep much these days. Unless you count the Council's disciplinary hearings. Then I'm out like a light."

Ren held up the scrap of paper. "This is new."

He plucked it from her fingers, examining it with a forensic intensity he usually reserved for Goodreads reviews of his books, or wine labels. "Handwriting analysis?" he offered, only half-joking.

She shook her head. "Never seen it. It wasn't here before."

Vincent's eyes flicked from the note to her arm, to her face, then back again. "Do you want to—" He broke off, the mask of sarcasm slipping just enough to show concern underneath. He tried again, gentler: "Is it hurting?"

Ren flexed her hand. The Mark responded with another pulse, then faded to a dull, resentful shimmer. "It's like the world's shittiest tattoo. I can feel it, even when I'm not looking."

Vincent made a non-committal noise. He didn't sit, but he leaned one hip on the edge of the bed, just far enough into her personal space to be protective, but not so close as to make her want to hit him.

He read the note aloud: "*The girl will fall in line, or she will fall apart.*" He smirked, but it didn't reach his eyes. "Subtle as ever."

Ren glared at the Mark, willing it to stop glowing, or maybe just to acknowledge her in some way that wasn't "harbinger of total collapse." "It's targeting me," she said. "Not you. Not Mrs Barley. Just... me. Again."

Vincent shrugged, but she could see the effort it took to play it off. "Maybe you're just more interesting."

She snorted. "You wish. If anyone here is prophecy bait, it's you."

He smiled, but she saw the fangs—barely exposed, the points white and sharp below his lip. "I was more the control group. You're clearly the better test case."

Ren balled her good hand into a fist. "Why now? It's been dormant for weeks."

He considered, then said, "Maybe Carmine's upped the dose. Or maybe it's responding to... external stimuli."

She rolled her eyes. "You mean me sleeping all day, eating nothing but Jaffa Cakes and trauma?"

He shrugged again, but this time it was almost a gesture of apology. "Could be. Or it's responding to something bigger."

They sat in silence, the light from her arm painting the bed in overlapping sickly halos. Ren realised she was shivering, but not from cold.

Vincent reached for the note again, this time flipping it over, as if the answer might be on the back. It was blank.

He pressed the scrap onto the bedside table with two fingers, pinning it in place. "If you want, I can call Zara. She's got her own methods for this sort of thing."

Ren shook her head. "Let her haunt in peace. She'll only make it weird."

He grinned, and this time it was real. "You say that like it's a bad thing."

Ren closed her eyes. The Mark itched, and she tried to ignore it, but the itch had become a pressure, like a hand slowly closing around her wrist. "What if it's not a prophecy anymore?" she asked, so quiet she wasn't sure she'd actually said it aloud.

Vincent considered, then said, "Then it's something worse."

She nodded, eyes still closed, and let herself lean back into the sofa, just enough to trust the world to not swallow her in the next five seconds. "You ever get scared?" she asked.

Vincent sipped his mug, and when he answered, his voice was almost gentle. "Every day. I just try not to show it."

Ren opened her eyes, and found him watching her, the concern now completely unmasked.

"Next time," she said, "bring me a coffee. And... thanks for staying, I appreciate it."

He held up his mug in a toast. "Next time, I'll bring the good stuff. Promise."

They sat in silence, the Mark pulsing quietly, the note flat and inert on the table, both of them pretending that the world hadn't just shifted under their feet.

In the kitchen, the fridge ticked over, humming its own little prophecy, and the city outside went on blinking, oblivious, towards the end of all things.

Zara arrived in the kitchen already halfway through a diagnosis, her spectral outline jittering at the edges like a dodgy Wi-Fi signal. She floated just above the tiled floor, arms folded, an expression of clinical interest on her see-through face.

"Let's have a look, then," she said, motioning for Ren to take the chair nearest the window.

Ren eyed the surface with suspicion. She'd watched Zara phase through it the previous night, and was ninety percent sure she'd left a quantum imprint of her arse behind, but she sat anyway. The Mark was still glowing, but now that the initial shock had faded, it felt less like an emergency and more like a very persistent notification.

Vincent loomed behind her, mug refilled and jaw set in that way that meant he was either spoiling for a fight or barely holding it together. Mrs Barley entered next, her posture perfect even in pyjamas, clipboard tucked under one arm and a fresh biro already poised for action.

Zara flicked into focus, conjuring a jeweller's loupe and a penlight from the ether. She addressed Ren's arm with a brisk, "Hold still," and began a series of passes with the loupe, tutting softly at each twist of the Mark.

"Not just an editor's seal anymore," she said. "And not a Council make, either. Look here—" She held Ren's arm just above the wrist, surprisingly solid for a ghost, and angled the loupe so the others could see. "It's iterative. Evolving. Whoever built this is running live code, not a static curse."

Ren's skin prickled, the Mark itching as if it resented being observed. "So, it's—what, learning?"

"Or updating," Zara replied. "Could be feedback from the network, could be a direct link to whoever set it. Either way, it's rewriting itself in response to you."

Vincent looked like he'd swallowed a battery. "But we destroyed the prophecy, the drafts, the words. You're telling me someone can remote-edit her from a distance?"

Zara handed the loupe to Mrs Barley, who examined the pattern and made a note. "It's a custom payload, Vincent," Zara said. "They can escalate, iterate, or burn it out whenever they want. The only reason it hasn't gone critical is—" She paused, tilting her head, "—you, probably. You're interfering with the process."

Ren tried for bravado. "Maybe I'm finally interesting," she said, but her hand shook as she tucked it into her hoodie pocket.

Zara leaned back—her version of giving space—and allowed Mrs Barley to complete a close inspection. "You're not in danger yet," Zara said. "But whoever's running this has a plan, and I'd bet the contents of my hard drive they're watching."

The silence was immediate, total.

It was Mrs Barley who broke it, voice soft and precise. "We need to isolate the signal. If it's networked, we can cut the feed. Or, at minimum, spoof the next update."

Vincent slumped against the counter, mug gripped in white-knuckle tension, not quite understanding the techno-babble. "Can you do it?"

Mrs Barley nodded, but her face said it would cost more than sleep. "I'll need time, and Zara's assistance. It's not like patching a leaky roof."

Ren exhaled. She hadn't realised she'd been holding her breath. The Mark's glow dimmed, but still cast a sickly shade across her lap.

Zara turned to Vincent, eyebrow raised. "You sure you're up for this? At the theatre, you ended up—well, almost dead."

He bared his fangs in what might have been a smile, but the edges were frayed. "I'm ready for Carmine."

Mrs Barley disappeared into the other room, returning

moments later with a tray: water for Ren, coffee for herself, a blood bag for Vincent. She set them down with the solemnity of a priest at the altar. The gesture was so ordinary, so mundane, it made the nightmare feel even more permanent.

Ren took the water and sipped, trying not to look at her arm. "I was hoping for a normal night," she said. "You know. Watch a bit of television, have a sandwich, not be a cypher for the end of the world."

Zara snorted. "Normal's overrated. Besides, if the Council ever finds out, you'll be famous. Or archived."

Ren managed a crooked smile, but the Mark flared then, sudden and violent, like someone had jabbed her with a live wire. She bit back a yelp as the pattern on her skin twisted, then re-wrote itself in three new segments, branching up toward the crook of her elbow.

The room's light flickered in sympathy. The fridge in the kitchen let out a tortured whine.

Vincent set down his mug, hand shaking just a little. "This isn't just happening again," he said, voice hoarse. "It's mutating."

They all stared at the Mark, watching it crawl and spiral over Ren's skin. Even Zara, who'd once watched her own body dissolve, looked unnerved.

Mrs Barley noted the changes, then looked up. "We'll keep monitoring. No one sleeps alone until we've figured out the update schedule."

Ren nodded, numb. Zara hovered closer, hand outstretched but not quite touching. Vincent, still standing, looked like he was about to start pacing, but the flat was too small for even that comfort.

For a long time, they just watched, four beings at the intersection of history, prophecy, and bad decisions, waiting for the next iteration to drop.

The Mark kept glowing, and outside, the night pressed in, silent and infinite, as if the world was waiting to see who would blink first.

SIX

Highgate Cemetery, in the hour after sunset, was a place that delighted in melodrama. The air dripped with enough moisture to breed entire new phyla of moss, and every third tree had an anecdote about Jack the Ripper. It was, in Vincent's estimation, the only locale in North London where the competition for Most Dramatic Entrance was stiff enough to put the Vampire Council to shame.

He picked his way along the gravel path, trench coat trailing like a stage curtain, and made for the statue garden at the centre of the older grounds. The sky was a sickly dark blue, the colour of old veins, and the mist had rolled in with the punctuality of a state funeral. Around him, marble cherubs and angels mourned at every conceivable angle, their blank stone eyes providing a thousand convenient places to avoid looking at the living.

Not that there were many living on hand, unless one counted the two souls meeting Vincent as part of the Council's "Nocturnal Outreach." Vincent, naturally, was the first to arrive, though only because insomnia and Council-mandated fieldwork were the only things that could get him out of the warmth of his flat in the winter.

He found his post: a crumbling plinth, topped by a willow-shouldered angel, her face permanently stuck in a state of exquisite regret. Vincent leaned against her base, lit a cigarette, and made a show of consulting his watch, which hadn't told the truth since the Thatcher era.

Mrs Barley arrived next, pursing her lips at the sight of Vincent's smouldering cigarette, then immediately ignoring it in favour of the night's operational checklist. She wore her standard surveillance kit—navy pea coat, grey gloves, scarf pinned with an unobtrusive Council sigil—and carried a battered picnic hamper that contained a large thermos, and an inordinate amount of stationery. Binoculars dangled from her neck, and her hair was, as ever, an architectural feat of pins and product.

She wasted no time in staking out her territory: a granite bench, conveniently dry, and positioned for optimal view of both the southern avenue and the open space where the "event" would presumably take place.

Ren was last, sprinting through the side gate and ducking behind a Celtic cross to catch her breath. Her cheeks were flushed in the cold, curls barely contained under a beanie. She clutched a spiral notebook to her chest and tried, valiantly, to look like someone who routinely surveilled supernatural subcultures at this hour.

Vincent greeted her with a wave, which she returned by raising two fingers, though whether in peace or insult was left ambiguous.

"I wasn't sure you'd come," he said, as she joined him at the statue.

Ren grunted. "They threatened to reassign me to the Camden Nephilim Watch if I didn't turn up. I don't even know what a Nephilim is."

Vincent pointed at the angel's downcast face. "Them, but with fewer scruples and worse taste in shoes."

Mrs Barley, already unpacking her arsenal of field forms and checklists, cut in. "If we're quite finished with the banter, I suggest we review our objectives. The Moderniser contingent is scheduled for a broadcast at precisely 19:51. If past patterns hold, they'll attempt to co-opt the local aesthetic for a new round of 'gothic night watch' streams."

Ren sidled up to get a look at the operational notes. "Is that a real thing? Do people actually watch vampires on YouTube?"

"It's not YouTube," Vincent said. "It's a custom platform. Something they cobbled together so they could monetise 'authentic undead content' without running afoul of the Council's copyright lawyers."

Ren made a face. "There's DMCA for bloodsuckers?"

"There's DMCA for everything," Mrs Barley replied, not looking up. She passed Ren a spare pair of binoculars and a packet of digestive biscuits. "Keep your phone on silent and your eyes on the principal targets. We're not to intervene, just observe and record. Understood?"

Vincent saluted, knowing it would annoy her. Ren nodded, mouth already half-full of biscuit.

They settled in to wait. The mist thickened, painting the statues in layers of pearl and grime. The only noise was the gentle patter of Ren scribbling in her notebook, and the even gentler patter of Vincent's sarcasm as he offered colour commentary on every passing squirrel, raven, or plastic bag.

Five minutes before showtime, the Modernisers arrived: a half-dozen youngbloods in expertly distressed black, their hair and makeup so flawless it could only be the result of collective narcissism or a sponsorship deal with a mortuary. They set up ring lights and folding tripods among the graves, moving with the choreographed confidence of people who had, in all likelihood, practised this in a rehearsal space.

Vincent snorted as one of the vampires, a lithe blond with boyband good looks, fussed over the angle of a reflector dish. "Babysitting influencers with better cheekbones than survival instincts. My career trajectory in a nutshell."

Ren took notes, pausing to snap a quick photo with her phone, which she immediately hid as one of the Modernisers glanced her way.

"I don't get it," she whispered. "If they're not supposed to exist, why the live broadcast?"

"Same reason a fungus releases spores," Vincent replied. "It's not about surviving, it's about being impossible to eradicate."

Mrs Barley watched the targets, eyes narrowed in concentration. "They're positioning themselves to ensure the full moon is in shot. At least four devices, possibly a drone on standby. If this is about glamour, it's overkill."

"They're Modernisers," Vincent said. "Overkill is their baseline."

The lead Moderniser, Aurelia Voss, took centre stage atop a particularly baroque tomb. Her outfit was an exquisite hybrid of high fashion and funeral attire, the hem dragging dramatically over the lichen. She made a short speech, which the sound tech (a surly-looking brunette with a nose ring) piped into the phones of her loyal viewers.

"Is she quoting Byron?" Ren asked, squinting at the livestream.

Vincent leaned in. "No, it's from her own memoir. She crowd-funded it last year. Hardcover, foil embossed title and sprayed edges. Two hundred pages of ramblings, interspersed with a selection of vegan recipes, four of them edible."

The Modernisers fanned out, filming each other in turn. The faux daylight of the ring lights turned everything the colour of blanched bone. Every so often, one would strike a pose with the statuary, or loll against a Victorian urn as if daring anyone to say "necro-chic" without irony.

At the perimeter, Zara Delacourt's ghost flickered into visibility, floating just above the line of headstones. She sank through a marble lamb, then reappeared atop a crypt, arms folded, looking for all the world like a very bored banshee.

She drifted toward Vincent's trio, voice echoing just enough to unsettle the less jaded. "You realise you're being watched by at least three other teams? The Council's got a side bet going on who'll snap first and just murder the lot."

Mrs Barley tensed, just a fraction. "We're here to observe, not intervene."

Zara grinned, a flash of phosphor in the haze. "Of course. I'm just here for the death tourism. Old habits."

Vincent addressed her over his shoulder, not breaking line of sight with the Modernisers. "You could have at least brought pastries. We're dying out here."

Zara drifted closer, flicking her spectral hair. "You think it's easy to buy almond croissants when you're dead? It's all gluten-free afterlife now."

Ren bit back a laugh, almost losing her grip on the binoculars. "You're not exactly a motivational speaker, are you?"

Zara shrugged. "I motivate people to leave the party before it gets weird. You should listen."

The Modernisers, meanwhile, were now fully immersed in their performance. On-screen, Aurelia raised her hands in a gesture of invocation, and the camera panned to capture the drama of the moment: a single, perfect tear tracking down her face, which the production assistant dabbed away between takes.

Vincent made a sound halfway between amusement and disgust. "There's more performance in that livestream than in all of Shakespeare."

"Not for long," Mrs Barley said, adjusting her binoculars. "They're starting the ritual segment."

The next three minutes proceeded with all the solemnity of a music awards acceptance speech. The Modernisers each recited a line of prepared script—something about remembering the old ways and honouring the past—then snapped open a bottle of faux-blood and poured it over a grave as if christening a particularly unlucky boat.

Ren took frantic notes. "This is... not what I expected."

Vincent grinned. "It's always a bit of a letdown when the supposed masters of darkness can't even vandalise a headstone without a product tie-in."

"Phase two," Mrs Barley murmured, "is where it usually goes sideways."

And it did. As the Modernisers circled the tomb for the

closing shot, something happened on the livestream. The captions, which had previously displayed harmless hashtags and quips, glitched. The screen flickered, then overlaid in a crimson text that did not match the font or branding of the Moderniser showrunners.

Vincent's breath hitched, a cold, familiar dread climbing his spine. "That's not their script," he said, eyes narrowing. "That's—"

On the viewer's phone, a new set of subtitles scrolled across: THE FUTURE FEEDS ON THE BLOOD OF THE FORGOTTEN. ALL STORIES REPEAT. HISTORY IS WRITTEN IN BONE.

Ren felt her stomach twist. "What is that?"

"Carmine," Vincent said, voice gone flat. "Or rather, Carmine's prophecy. But it's... leaking."

Mrs Barley, ever the professional, clicked her biro and began to record the anomaly, but her hand froze mid-sentence. On her own tablet, the Council-issue surveillance app began to glitch. The screen flashed, then displayed the same text, over and over, each repetition a little more frantic, a little more insistent.

THE FUTURE FEEDS. THE FUTURE FEEDS. THE FUTURE FEEDS.

Ren checked her phone, only to find that every app, every window, every possible way of contacting the outside world had been hijacked by the same message, scrolling in blood-red, impossible to close.

Vincent spat a curse, flicked his cigarette into the grass. "He's breached the digital. It's not just us anymore."

Zara hovered just above the ground, voice barely above a whisper. "I told you. The party always ends weird."

They all watched, helpless, as the Modernisers continued their performance, oblivious to the fact that the real show had already started, and the audience was now the entire waking world.

The moon reached its zenith, painting the cemetery in a sickly, unreal light. The statues wept their stone tears, the mist clung to everything, and above it all, the prophecy scrolled on, bright and horrible and unstoppable.

Vincent closed his eyes, just for a second, and imagined what Carmine would have said.

Probably: "Told you so."

He opened his eyes, squared his shoulders, and looked to Mrs Barley and Ren. "We need to warn the Council. Now."

Mrs Barley was already on it, thumb stabbing the emergency contact, jaw set. Ren, pale, just nodded, then reached for her phone again, as if the next message might be less terrifying.

Zara watched them, a half-smile on her not-quite-there face. "Good luck," she said, already drifting backwards into the mist. "You'll need it."

The first notifications started to ping in the city below. Hashtags exploded. Videos went viral. And in the graveyard, under the first indifferent moonlight, the Modernisers kept filming, believing they'd started the future.

They had. Just not the one anyone wanted.

The instant the Modernisers wrapped their "ritual segment," a change rippled through the graveyard that had nothing to do with lighting or weather. It started as a flicker in the corner of the eye; the kind of subtle warp that made every stone angel look a fraction too animate and every lichen-stained cross tilt one degree more oblique.

Then the epitaphs began to glow.

It was subtle at first—a faint, infra-red shimmer in the grooved letters of every headstone within sight. But within seconds, the light intensified, bleeding up through the cracks and moss until every grave in the cemetery blazed with an unholy scarlet, as if the entire Necropolis had decided to turn on its hazard lights.

Ren, normally unflappable, dropped her notebook. The impact echoed in the silence, drawing the eyes of the Modernisers and their cameramen, who all paused in unison to gawp at the phenomenon.

Vincent watched, a slow smile carving itself onto his face. "Showtime," he said, almost to himself.

On cue, the epitaphs began to liquefy. Carved letters sagged and sloughed like wax left on a radiator, pooling into the grooves and then draining down the face of the stone. For a full three seconds, the grave markers wept lines of black-and-red sludge, which pooled at their bases before, impossibly, reforming into new text.

Ren managed to read the first line aloud, voice trembling: "FEED THE FUTURE. BLEED THE PAST."

"Carmine," Vincent confirmed, fangs peeking from his grin. "That bastard never did know when to leave well enough alone."

From somewhere behind them, a Moderniser shrieked—not a mortal terror shriek, but the shriek of a content creator who had just seen their subscriber count triple. Ring lights swivelled, phones tilted, and within seconds every angle of the new horror was being live-broadcast to an audience already primed for melodrama.

Mrs Barley, unamused, thumbed open her emergency kit and palmed a length of silver chain, which she wound around one gloved hand like rosary beads. "Remember, do not expose yourself to direct viral projection. If you must engage, keep it offline."

Vincent cocked an eyebrow. "You realise the only people not filming are us?"

Mrs Barley shot him a glare that could have frozen the Thames. "You can edit your memoirs later."

At the far end of the angel garden, a grave marker buckled with a deep, wet crack, sending up a plume of grave-dust and ground beetles. Something clawed out—a hand, or what was left of one, sinew wrapped tight around bone, every finger tipped with nails that glittered in the red light.

Ren backpedalled, colliding with Vincent. "You said this wasn't your kind of prophecy," she hissed.

"It's not," he whispered, eyes fixed on the grave. "This is Carmine's stunt. But he's using my goddamn script."

The thing that rose from the grave was not a Moderniser. It was older, and hungrier, and so thoroughly decayed it looked like someone had tried to taxidermy a murder. Its face was a parody of the aristocratic, stretched too long, lips split to reveal yellow, root-like fangs. It wore the shreds of a Victorian suit, now black with earth and rot, and as it clawed free of the grave, it screamed a single line:

"HISTORY IS WRITTEN IN BLOOD."

This was apparently the trigger for the rest of the cemetery. One by one, the graves broke open, each vomiting forth a revenant—a pale, ruined parody of the vampires that had once held dominion over this part of London. They came in every style and epoch: Edwardians with cravats glued to their throats, flappers with hair matted into a single wet braid, Sixties Mods in suits now reeking of ammonia and rot. Each one's face was wrong in a way that made Ren's vision strobe, as if they'd been assembled from rejected police sketches and urban legends.

Vincent stepped forward, fangs fully extended now, voice low and lethal. "Mrs Barley. Take Ren and find cover."

"I am not leaving you—"

"Not a request."

He didn't wait to see if they obeyed, because the first wave of revenants was already on him. They moved with a jerky, marionette rhythm, arms windmilling and jaws clacking open and shut as they screamed the prophecy in perfect, multilingual unison.

Vincent met them head-on, fists and feet and fangs in a flurry of violence so raw it bordered on obscene. Every impact cracked a revenant's skull or snapped a rotten limb, sending up plumes of dust and bone chips that settled on the grass like filthy confetti. The Modernisers filmed it all, faces oscillating between horror and glee.

"Vincent!" Ren screamed, from behind a toppled angel. "There's too many!"

"Not yet," he called back, grabbing the nearest revenant by the lapels and headbutting it so hard its cranium collapsed. "But I'll let you know."

Three more closed in, claws raking Vincent's back, one

managing to sink its teeth into his shoulder. He yanked it free, tearing out a clump of its own jaw in the process. "Did you know," he grunted, "the Victorians used to bury these with iron cages? Ahead of their time, really."

Ren and Mrs Barley huddled behind the angel, both watching in mounting panic as Vincent was rapidly encircled. Mrs Barley, refusing to cower, unsheathed her umbrella and twisted the handle. The tip gleamed with newly exposed silver.

"If you're going to do something," Ren muttered, "now is good."

Mrs Barley nodded, then broke cover, moving with a speed that belied her age. She jabbed the umbrella into a revenant's eye socket, then used it as leverage to spin the creature into a headstone, which promptly shattered under the impact.

Ren, realising she was next to useless in hand-to-hand combat, fumbled through the emergency kit and found a marine rescue flare. She thumbed off the safety and fired it into the largest cluster of revenants. The flare ignited mid-arc, painting the mob in apocalyptic red and scattering them long enough for Vincent to break free.

"Nice shot," he called, ducking as a revenant tried to take his head off with a chunk of masonry.

"Xbox," Ren gasped, "Call of Duty."

Above the chaos, Zara's ghost bobbed and weaved through the air, shrieking directions:

"Left, Vincent! No, your other left! Ren, duck! Oh, never mind, you're doing fine, just don't die."

Mrs Barley, umbrella now slick with blackish ooze, drove the point into another revenant's throat, then flicked it free with an expert wrist twist. "Improper resurrection protocol," she muttered, "violation of Section 17B, and don't even get me started on the dress code."

Vincent, shirt torn and bleeding, was running out of stamina. He tore a leg off a toppled statue and used it to club the nearest revenant into a spray of wet gravel. "I could use a little help here!" he shouted.

Zara, swooping low, passed her non-corporeal hand through the nearest revenant's skull. The effect was instantaneous: the creature froze, then toppled to the ground, shuddering as its internal circuitry rebooted to "off." She looked briefly pleased with herself, then frowned. "Doesn't work on all of them," she called down. "Some are firewall protected!"

Ren, ducking another revenant, tripped over her own notebook and landed hard on the grass. Her arm—the one with the Mark—flared with sudden, burning pain. The tattoo writhed, then projected a ring of light outward, slicing cleanly through the ankle of the revenant that was about to land on her. The creature faceplanted into the dirt, shrieking all the way.

She stared at her arm in shock, then at the fallen creature. "Did I just—?"

Vincent grinned, even as he crushed a revenant's skull beneath his boot. "Looks like you've been upgraded."

The fight lasted another minute, maybe less, before the last of the revenants collapsed into a puddle of rot and vintage polyester. The red glow from the epitaphs faded, replaced by the cold, dark black of night.

Vincent, panting and spitting grave dirt, leaned against a toppled headstone. His knuckles were raw, shirt torn open to reveal a dozen new scars already knitting closed. "Well," he said, voice shot. "That was dramatic."

Ren crawled over, bleeding from one arm, the Mark still pulsing but softer now. "You okay?"

He glanced down at his ruined clothes and the heap of dead things at his feet. "I've been worse. Once. Maybe twice."

Mrs Barley joined them, umbrella dripping with ichor, eyes cold and professional. She surveyed the carnage with a calm born of centuries spent cleaning up after idiots, and more recently, Vincent. "We need to decontaminate. Council won't want this going viral."

Ren blinked, then pointed at the nearest Moderniser, who was still filming, even as she tried to wipe blood off her phone screen.

"Too late," Ren said, voice cracking into a laugh. "It's already everywhere."

Vincent staggered upright and peered over the graves toward the angel garden, where the Modernisers were busy conducting a victory lap for their followers. In the distance, a drone buzzed, catching aerial shots of the aftermath.

He turned to Mrs Barley. "Council's going to love this."

Mrs Barley just sighed. "I'll draft a memo."

Zara hovered over the group, hair still sparking with aftershocks. "You know what's trending right now?" she asked. "#ZombieHighgate and #VampireApocalypse. Also, 'why is my arm glowing,' but that might be just you, Ren."

Ren cradled her arm, which was already starting to itch again. "At least we're famous."

Mrs Barley, already on the phone to the Council, recited the incident report in the clipped monotone of someone who had long ago ceased to be shocked by anything. "Containment failed. Targets multiplied. Prophecy manifest. Awaiting further instruction."

Vincent watched as the Modernisers wrapped up their broadcast, giddy with their own survival. In the city below, notifications were already lighting up, every social feed abuzz with rumours, videos, and the kind of theories that could only be generated by people who'd never seen a real monster in their lives.

He wiped the blood from his mouth and smiled, just a little. "I don't know about you, but I think I deserve a drink."

Ren grinned, and for a moment, even Mrs Barley looked like she might be on the verge of something resembling laughter.

They limped off together, leaving the graves to settle and the city to do what it did best: bury the truth under a mountain of memes.

As they vanished into the fog, Zara drifted after, her voice echoing over the ruined stones. "Next time, I'm bringing the croissants."

No one disagreed.

SEVEN

By sunrise, the city had regurgitated everything it couldn't process the night before. Highgate's southern perimeter was choked with news vans, their satellite dishes angled in rigid semaphore, relaying live coverage of the scene to a public with an infinite appetite for spectacle and no patience for context. The pavement outside the main gate crawled with reporters, each one carefully calibrated for maximum piety or maximum outrage, depending on whether they were billing the story as "Community in Shock" or "Cult Ritual Gone Wrong." Police tape hung limp across the gates, mostly decorative, since anyone motivated enough to break in would find only a slurry of revenant mud and a few broken gravestones.

Vincent, Ren, and Mrs Barley watched the circus on the television. Vincent had not changed clothes, on principle. The bloodstains had faded to sepia, but his face still bore the fine grit of the previous night's grave-dirt, and his left knuckle was bandaged with something that had started life as a receipt. He looked like a man who had not only lost a fight, but had done so with a running commentary and a complete disregard for the odds.

Ren scrolled through her phone, thumb flicking with professional velocity. "We're up to one-point-four-million views," she reported, not bothering to hide the grim satisfaction in her voice. "Hashtag #ZombieHighgate has an official merch store now. You can get the t-shirts in black or 'corpse white'."

"Lovely," Vincent said, eyes fixed on the TV. "And to think, the Council spent the better part of a century making sure Highgate was only haunted by tragic poets and the occasional fascist."

Mrs Barley, immune to sarcasm, sipped from her cup of tea. "What are the newspapers saying?"

Ren called up some apps on her phone and handed it to Mrs Barley, who squinted at the display with a mixture of dread and hunger.

"They're calling it a 'mass hallucination event,'" Ren reported. "Also: 'possible cult cosplay flashmob.' The official police line is that a group of 'social media pranksters' vandalised the cemetery with home-made special effects. But there's already a petition to have all the graves exhumed. For... verification."

Vincent snorted. "It's always the exhumation. Never just 'bad dreams' and move on."

Behind the reporter on TV, a van with "GMB" in huge letters slammed into the kerb, nearly taking out two tabloid photographers and a woman in a trench coat who, judging by her posture, was a detective or at least paid to play one on the BBC. The rear doors opened, disgorging a camera crew who immediately set up shop five metres from the tape, aiming their lens directly at the cemetery gates.

"Nothing says cover-up like an ITV news van," Vincent muttered.

Mrs Barley flinched at the word "cover-up," as if the mere mention could summon Council strike teams. She held out her phone so Vincent could see the trending clips. One was a heavily filtered video of the revenant brawl, the reds cranked to eleven, so the whole screen looked like it had been filmed through a blood droplet. The user commentary was a nested war of accusations, some claiming it was "obviously a TV drama pilot," others debating which branch of cryptid taxonomy the things in the video belonged to.

Vincent watched for a moment, then said, "They're not even getting the fangs right. If you're going to doctor the footage, at least use a reference photo."

"They're not even arguing about whether it's real anymore," Ren said. "Just what kind of real it is."

Ren, squinting at the television screen, clicked her fingers. "Is that—are those the Council's clean-up crew?"

Vincent followed her gaze. Behind the reporter, two figures in high-viz jackets, one of whom was already wheeling a pressure washer toward the main avenue. The other held a clipboard and a bucket marked "Hazmat—Type III," and was reading a laminated checklist with the intensity of a surgeon prepping for a triple bypass.

"Not Council," Mrs Barley corrected, with absolute authority. "That's outsourced. Private firm. The Council would never use a public-facing vehicle."

Vincent eyed the crew with mild interest. "Shows how seriously they're taking this," he said. "The last time there was a leak this big, they shut down three postcodes and flooded the sewers with bleach."

"Maybe they're just going to let it burn out," Zara suggested, arms folded. "Like the Blitz, or gonorrhoea."

A silence settled, heavy and a little sour.

Mrs Barley's hands worked the edge of her phone, blanching her knuckles. "The Council will be livid," she said, voice pitched so low it barely cleared the memorial. "This is more than a breach. This is a... a narrative collapse."

Vincent's lips curled, not quite a smile. "Good," he said. "Let them choke on it."

"You think they'll try to memory-wipe everyone?" Ren asked.

Mrs Barley shook her head, eyes fixed on the ground. "Too late. It's already viral. They'd have to erase half of London, and even then—"

"Even then, someone would sell the story," Vincent finished. "London loves a good ghost story. And now it's got a whole new cast."

They sat together, watching as every media organisation adjusted, adapted, metabolised the horror and spat it back out as a five-minute segment on breakfast TV." The new normal, updated daily.

Ren broke the silence, voice almost gentle. "You ever feel like we're just extras in someone else's drama?"

"Constantly," Vincent said. "But at least the catering's good."

Mrs Barley straightened her cardigan, squaring her shoulders in that way she had, as if every fresh disaster was a personal affront. "We'll have to report in," she said, already rehearsing the apology in her head. "The Council will want... statements."

Vincent snorted. "They can have mine in writing. Less risk of me biting someone's head off."

The Council chamber was colder than the last time, as if the building itself had decided to contribute to the sense of imminent execution. The lights had been dialled down to "funeral," and the air hummed with the psychic tension of two dozen immortals, none of whom had slept since the news cycle began.

Vincent stood at the foot of the dais, a position that would have been humiliating if he cared about things like dignity. Ren was beside him, hands jammed in her pockets, this time her gaze fixed on a spot somewhere between her shoes and the ceiling. Mrs Barley completed the triangle, posture so correct she seemed to be holding up the rest of the room by sheer force of etiquette.

At the head of the chamber, Elder Blackthorn paced behind his desk, ancient robes swishing in a manner that might have been theatrical if it hadn't also been genuinely threatening. Every few steps, he paused to jab a clawed finger at the screen behind him, where a rolling projection cycled through news coverage, social media highlights, and a looping montage of the night's carnage, scored to the kind of string music that usually signalled either a nature documentary or a war crime tribunal.

"This," Blackthorn thundered, "is the result of your gross mismanagement."

He stabbed the gavel down, hard enough to dent the oak. The chamber reverberated.

"Mortals believe in revenants now. Do you understand the exposure? There are calls for exhumation, for DNA testing, for bloody public inquiries."

Another elder, a woman with a face like a cracked vase and the voice to match, interrupted: "They have named it! 'Zombie Highgate.' It is a meme! Is this what you intended, Lupo?"

Vincent shrugged. "The hashtags were out of my hands."

"Nothing was out of your hands," Blackthorn snapped. "You were tasked with monitoring the Modernisers, not starring in their viral campaign. Instead, you have—" he waved toward the screen, where Zara's ghostly form now trended alongside the Council's own logo, "—become the meme."

There was a collective hiss of displeasure from the benches.

Vincent let the silence stretch, then stepped forward, squaring his battered shoulders. "Maybe the problem isn't us," he said, "but you letting the prophecy leak all over London."

The Council erupted. For a second, it seemed the eldritch containment wards would rupture from sheer volume. One of the proxies in the back row lost structural integrity and sagged into its neighbour, who caught it with the resigned efficiency of someone who had cleaned up much worse.

"You dare blame the Council?" Blackthorn roared. "When you alone failed to—"

"—failed to what?" Vincent shot back. "Pretend it wasn't happening? That's your entire doctrine. If you can't stick it in a report, you ignore it."

Another elder—Grenville, possibly, though it was hard to tell when his nose was fully submerged in the archives—

rose to his feet and bellowed, "We have maintained secrecy for centuries. We have survived pogroms, inquisitions, wars! And you would throw it away for... for what? A headline?"

"Secrecy's already broken," Vincent said, voice low. "You're just the last to know."

Ren, who had up to this point played the role of silent chorus, coughed. "It's not going to stop, you know. Even if you vanish us. It's already out. People want to believe in monsters, and now they have proof."

She received a look of such withering contempt from a hundred-year-old councilwoman that her hair nearly frizzed from the force of it.

Blackthorn rounded on Mrs Barley. "And you, the supposed brains of the operation among this collection of failures, what do you say in your defence?"

Mrs Barley's voice, when it came, was so composed it bordered on clinical detachment. "Containment was impossible after the first viral event. Suppressing it now would require either a complete digital blackout or an unprecedented mass memory edit. Both would produce their own anomalies, and risk further exposure. My recommendation is controlled narrative adjustment."

Blackthorn scowled, but she pressed on: "You can't erase this. But you can curate it. Lean into the performance. Make it a fiction, and the world will believe what you tell it to."

There was a long pause. The council, unaccustomed to having its options reduced to "accept defeat" or "go full psyop," seemed briefly at a loss.

Vincent glanced at Ren, then at the bench where Zara was

now doing a ghostly handstand, ignoring the proceedings with a professional's contempt for bureaucracy.

Blackthorn recovered, and brought down the gavel again. "If you insist on making noise, Lupo, we will have no choice but to erase you. Comprehensively. There are fates far worse than death. Do not test us."

Vincent opened his mouth, but for once, found nothing he wanted to say. Instead, he nodded, a tiny, fatalistic bow.

The council adjourned with a flurry of pronouncements and the kind of ceremonial glares that could curdle milk. Blackthorn lingered as the rest filed out, eyes never leaving Vincent's face.

When the chamber finally emptied, Mrs Barley, Ren, and Vincent trudged together down the corridor, their footsteps echoing in the sepulchral quiet.

Ren broke the silence, voice small but unafraid. "If they won't stop it, who will?"

Vincent walked a few more paces before answering, his jaw so tight it might have been wired shut. "I don't know," he said, voice raw. "But we're not out of options yet."

Mrs Barley, not breaking stride, made a note in her book. "There's always a loophole," she said, almost to herself.

They walked on, the underground tunnels closing behind them like the throat of a very old, very hungry god.

EIGHT

Zara's flat, thanks to Ren's habitation, abandoned any remaining pretence at being habitable and instead went straight for the aesthetic of a historian's deathbed. Not a single surface was free of detritus: books in triplicate, folders gnawed by silverfish, take-out boxes evolving their own symbiotic cultures, and at the centre of the mess, a battered pine table that had seen both the Victorian spiritualist boom and the 1970s rent strike, judging by the spectrum of candle wax and ballpoint graffiti embedded in its grain.

Twilight seeped through the grime of the windows, painting everything with that tragic, pre-electric blue. The city's noise came in muffled, like the world had been demoted to a supporting character, and the only real movement was the slow drift of dust and the occasional tremble from the overworked washing machine.

Around the table, Mrs Barley and Ren were already hard at it, sleeves rolled, fingers blackened with the ink of centuries.

They worked with opposing strategies: Mrs Barley methodical and lethal, collating and annotating the Council's dossiers with the precision of a pathologist, Ren attacking her stack in brief, caffeine-fuelled spurts, sticky notes multiplying on her side like fungal growth.

Vincent, meanwhile, had claimed the sofa—more springs than upholstery, but still the closest thing to a throne the flat had to offer. He sprawled there with theatrical exhaustion, glass of red sloshing from one hand, the other making desultory sweeps through the latest printout of the Moderniser livestreams. The bottle—Rioja, on special—sat open at his side, never more than an arm's reach away, and as dusk thickened, so did his absorption in the drink.

Zara herself was, as ever, the most kinetic presence in the flat, despite being the only one not technically alive. She flickered in and out of visibility, sometimes phasing straight through the stacks of books, other times manifesting at full intensity to hurl a pencil at Ren's head or to roll her eyes at one of Vincent's more defeatist pronouncements. She moved with the energy of a teenager on her sixth Red Bull, and though her preferred state was a mild, ghostly haze, whenever she found something that interested her, she popped into three-dimensional existence so abruptly it made the lightbulbs stutter.

She was doing exactly that now, head and shoulders emerging from a pile of Council files on the far side of the table. Her eyes shone with the specific madness of someone who had not only looked into the abyss, but taken notes and annotated them.

"Look at this," she said, voice echoing more in the ears than the air. "Carmine's own notes for the prophecy, before his lordship over there was employed to ghostwrite the thing—there's always a deleted line at the midpoint. Not redacted. Deleted. Like someone ripped out a paragraph and then pretended it was never there."

Mrs Barley, who had reached that point of paperwork inebriation where even her hair bun was drooping, snapped to alertness. She slid a Council issue monocle from her breast pocket and held it up to the parchment, the glass haloed with protective sigils.

"Confirmed," she said, after a moment's scan. "Marginalia suggests intentional removal, not accident. And see this—" she tapped a biro against the margin, "—there's an editorial mark here, old style. Like a proofreader's check, but not human."

Vincent, who had been content to let the others do the heavy lifting, finally sat up. "Let me guess. Carmine's handwriting?"

Zara grinned, shifting her spectral form until she hovered a good inch over the table. "Bingo. The bastard edited each draft. Every time he sent one out into the wild, he rewrote it. Sometimes it's just a word, sometimes a whole stanza. But it's always there, the same mark."

Ren, who was trying to both keep up and not pass out from the effort, scribbled notes at triple speed. "So, he's... versioning his own apocalypse?"

Zara nodded. "It's iterative. Like code. Or fanfic, if your fandom is 'the end of the world'. It's not yet as powerful as the draft Vincent wrote, but it's learning. Adapting. Growing into its own potential. He's tweaking multiple versions at the same time.'"

Vincent's lips curled, but it was more snarl than smile. "And the sum is greater than the parts."

A wind must have gotten in somewhere, because all at once the candles along the windowsill guttered, plunging the room into a flickering half-dark. The change in light made Zara's outline flare with blue, casting a death-mask glow across the piles of research. She took full advantage, scooping a scatter of papers from the table and fanning them with a flourish.

"What's really fun," she said, voice pitched up into the brittle register of a substitute teacher on her last nerve, "is that each deleted line has a shadow. You can't see it in the original ink, but if you go spectral—" she phased her hand through the sheet, leaving it briefly translucent, "—it glows. Like there's a ghost of the missing text."

Mrs Barley adjusted her glasses, peering at the page. "You mean it's encoded?"

"More like haunted," said Zara. "You ever see a dead document? It's like a fossil, or a scar. And these prophecies—" she jabbed at the air, making the documents shiver, "—are riddled with them. Carmine didn't just write history. He kept trying to erase it. And every time, it came back meaner."

Vincent drained his glass. "He's the writer who won't die. Literally."

Zara shot him finger guns, which somehow worked even without fingers. "Exactly."

Ren, wide-eyed and slightly glazed, tapped her pen against her teeth. "Can you recover the missing bits?"

Zara's grin widened. "Can and have, darling. Spent most of this week in the Archive, cross-referencing every bootlegged version, every Council transcript, every Moderniser meme. It's all here." She swept a hand toward the mess, and, for a moment, every piece of paper on the table shimmered and reorganised itself, stacking and restacking in patterns only Zara could see.

The effect was so strange that even Vincent blinked. "That's... new."

"Poltergeist life-hack," Zara said, flashing a smile. "But look—here, and here, and here." She pointed out three places on three different documents. "Same mark. Same phrase, deleted every time: 'The final draft will be perfect.'"

Ren scribbled the line, then shuddered. "That's what the Council called our little outing at the Orpheum, right? The 'Perfected Prophecy.'"

Mrs Barley nodded, jaw set. "I thought we burned every last scrap."

Vincent looked at the papers, then at the others. "We did. Of my version, anyway."

"But we didn't destroy the original notes and drafts," said Zara.

Silence.

The washing machine went into a spin cycle, and the whole flat seemed to lean in, as if expecting a punchline that didn't arrive.

Mrs Barley, taking refuge in the language of bureaucracy, tapped her pen against the dossier. "Now we have the iterations, we can reconstruct the full payload. Maybe even anticipate the next update."

Vincent gestured at the bottle, which was now a third lower than it had been. "Unless Carmine's already written it. In which case, we're just playing catchup."

Zara shrugged. "Either way, we have more data than the

Council ever did. And if Carmine's still pushing updates, maybe we can get ahead of him for once."

Ren looked up from her notes. "You think we can finish the draft before he does?"

Zara's eyes sparkled with mischief and a little fear. "I think we can at least read the ending before the world does."

Vincent, who had spent the whole conversation trying to look unaffected, suddenly went very still. He looked at the document in front of him, the faint ghost script that danced on the surface, and for a moment, he seemed less a vampire and more a man who had spent too long chasing a past that refused to stay dead.

"He always said he'd have the last word," Vincent muttered, almost to himself.

Zara nodded, and the candles guttered again, leaving them all in blue-shadowed silence.

The prophecy fragments glimmered on the table, and the city outside held its breath, waiting for the next draft.

The table, already burdened with centuries of doom, now bore an even greater load: Zara had arranged the prophecy fragments in a careful, deliberate spiral, each tattered scrap overlapping the next, ends and beginnings stitched together with ghost-light. The effect was less "puzzle" and more "crime scene," as if the prophecy had suffered a series of traumatic deaths and every piece was its own murder weapon.

Vincent regarded the spiral with the weary suspicion of a

man who had once spent six years auditing the Council's backlog of "uncontainable" archives. He poured himself a second glass, the glug of wine loud in the hush that had settled after Zara's last revelation.

Ren watched from her seat, arms curled tight around her knees, eyes darting from fragment to fragment. Her notepad was now less a notebook and more a nervous system—lines everywhere, crossing and doubling back, each diagram more frantic than the last.

Mrs Barley alone seemed undaunted by the occult spectacle. She donned her silver-rimmed spectacles—a relic from her time serving edicts, rumoured to be forged from reclaimed Council excommunication tokens—and leaned in, tracing the spiral with a finger.

Zara hovered above the fray, her spectral form condensed to a silhouette so sharp it hurt to look at directly. She gestured to the table, voice echoing in stereo. "Each draft ends differently. But look—" She phased her hand through the central cluster, scattering a fine mist of afterimage, "—every single one has Carmine's name. Here, here, here." Each point shimmered blue as she touched it.

Ren squinted at a particularly ragged fragment, where the ink had bled and re-bled through the page, as if it was fighting to escape. "He signs the prophecy? That's so—"

"On brand?" Vincent offered, without humour.

"Pathological," Mrs Barley corrected, straightening the page with two brisk flicks. "He isn't leaving a signature. He's leaving a hash. Each iteration is a checksum for the next."

Zara clapped, delighted. "See? I knew you'd get it. It's not a prophecy. It's a version history."

Mrs Barley, energised now, started reordering the fragments, her movements crisp and mathematical. "If we treat these as code, each change is a patch. A bug fix. The deleted lines are deprecated functions. The new lines are updates."

Ren watched as Mrs Barley lined up two nearly identical fragments, then adjusted them so their edges formed a perfect seam. When she pressed them together, the text on both flickered, then—impossibly—resolved into a third, more complete stanza.

Mrs Barley sat back, a look of vindication on her face. "Iterative recursion. Each version cannibalises the last. He's trying to achieve... something like narrative singularity."

Vincent's grip on his glass whitened. "But why? What's the point of rewriting the end of the world over and over?"

Zara drifted lower, eye-level now with the table. "Because if you write the final draft, you get to decide what the ending is. Carmine's trying to overwrite reality. Not with magic—" She grinned, savage, "—but with editorial control."

The words hung in the air, dense as incantation.

Ren shivered, and only then did she notice the heat crawling up her arm. The Editor's Mark, dormant for days, was pulsing faintly—its blue-green glow now synced to the rhythm of the prophecy on the table. Each time Mrs Barley shifted a fragment, the light in the Mark flickered in perfect time.

She yanked her sleeve down, but not before Vincent noticed. "Well, that's new. Or is it?"

Ren managed, "It's reacting. I don't know why."

Zara leaned in, the edge of her sleeve blending into the table. "Because you're part of the story now. You're the next patch."

Vincent set his glass down, very carefully. "Great. Not only is it mutating, it's got a fan club."

Mrs Barley, unperturbed, pushed her glasses up her nose. "If Carmine is still alive—"

"Definitely not alive," Zara interrupted. "He's undead, or close enough. Half-in, half-out. Every time his words go viral, every time someone reads the next iteration, he gets stronger. More present."

Vincent gave a hollow laugh. "So, every idiot livestreaming the Moderniser meltdown is bringing him back?"

"Not back," said Zara. "He never left. He's just waiting for the right moment to rewrite himself in."

For a long moment, the only sound was the hum of the fridge, the sizzle of a candle burning too close to its own label, and the city outside, suddenly distant.

Mrs Barley looked to Ren. "How do you feel?"

Ren flexed her hand, watched the Mark pulse once, twice, then settle. "Like something's updating me. I keep getting... lines. In my head. Not thoughts, just—syntax. Rewriting itself."

Zara nodded, solemn. "He's using you as a test environment. You're the vessel. Again."

Vincent stood, sudden and abrupt, knocking his glass to the floor. It rolled under the sofa and bled out onto the ancient carpet.

"No," he said. "He's not getting the last word. Not this time."

Zara regarded him, eyes flat and old. "You can't outwrite him, Vincent. He edits from the root."

Mrs Barley, ever the voice of reason, said, "Then we need to break the chain. Stop the next update before it propagates."

Zara's smile was sharp as a scalpel. "You'll need to go to the source."

Ren's head jerked up. "You know where Carmine is?"

Zara didn't answer directly, but drifted to the window, looking out over the city. "He's wherever the story is loudest. Wherever people are hungry for an ending."

Mrs Barley squared her shoulders, already planning. "We'll need access to the Council's deep vaults. That must be where the original Carmine drafts are kept. If we can roll back the prophecy—"

"—we might be able to overwrite the overwrite," Vincent finished, catching on.

And in the silence, the Mark on Ren's arm began to rewrite itself, line by line, in perfect time with Carmine's ghost.

NINE

Elder Mortimer Blackthorn presided, as always, from a throne that implied "autocracy" even when unoccupied. He wore his robes like he'd never found a use for the word "casual," and his fingers spidered over the desk with a steady, syncopated loathing. Around him, other Council immortals exchanged micro-expressions: tight lips, eye rolls, a flick of tongue at a canine. The proxies in the back row did their best "flesh-coloured waxwork" routine, but even they seemed bored.

Mrs Barley cleared her throat and addressed the room with the authority of a headmistress confronting an Ofsted inspection gone satanic. "The purpose of this emergency session," she said, "is to present evidence of an active, evolving narrative threat within the London Moderniser population. The findings are... unconventional."

She set Zara's dossier in the centre of the Council table. The cover sheet read "PROPHECY ITERATION EVENT:

CANDIDATE CARMINE," under which Zara had scrawled a smiley face with vampire fangs.

"Begin," Blackthorn said, voice tuned for maximum bleakness.

Mrs Barley flicked her tablet to the first page, which displayed three annotated prophecy drafts, all dated within the last two weeks. "Council will note that each Moderniser incident is preceded by a variant of the Carmine Prophecy—subtle changes in syntax, line order, or metaphoric load. In every instance, the edits bear unique marginalia: an editorial mark not matching any known Council or human hand."

The screens flickered, revealing blown-up scans of the deleted lines. In the margins, a distinct hash repeated, like the signature of an overzealous software update. Beside each, a forensic close-up showed where the original ink had "bled" into a spectral afterimage.

Vincent leaned in, unable to resist. "This is his MO. He's running a bloody narrative virus, and the Modernisers are the petri dish."

A councilwoman with a jawline like an anvil raised an eyebrow. "And your evidence that the—" she squinted at her monitor, "—'deleted lines' are not merely poetic affect?"

Mrs Barley bristled. "Because each deletion recurs, with increasing aggression, across every recorded outbreak. Further, spectral analysis reveals Carmine's own residual imprint at the scene—his 'fingerprint' in the ink."

Blackthorn cut in. "And you expect the Council to act on the say-so of a poltergeist?"

Zara, flickering in a side alcove and visible only to the very bored and the very dead, flipped a ghostly two-fingered salute. Nobody on the bench even acknowledged her.

Vincent's grip tightened around his sheaf of notes, wine-stain showing at the wrist. "Maybe if your own Council archivists hadn't buried the last Carmine event under three tonnes of red tape and bleach, we wouldn't be getting our next apocalypse in serialised instalments."

The councilwoman smirked, scribbling on a physical pad as if to reinforce the point. "There is still no direct evidence of Carmine's return, only—what was the term?—ghost gossip."

"Ghosts have never lied to you before," Vincent snapped, "except for the times you paid them to."

Ren, meanwhile, was trying to keep her head down, but the Mark on her forearm had started to hum with a weird, dental-drill urgency. She pressed her sleeve against it, hoping the Council's interest in the metaphysical had atrophied along with their sense of self-preservation.

Mrs Barley, sensing the way the tide was going, shifted from science to policy. "With respect, Elder Blackthorn, this is not a speculative threat. Carmine's influence is escalating. If the prophecy reaches full recursion, we'll be looking at an event on the scale of the New Cross Massacre—possibly worse."

There was a pause, then a chorus of desk drumming from the proxies: the Council's version of "don't be so bloody dramatic." Vincent braced for a monologue.

Blackthorn did not disappoint. "Mrs Barley, you have served the Council with distinction for decades. But this? This is not evidence. This is the fever dream of a dead archivist, abetted by an overzealous vampire with a Messiah complex and a junior investigator who can't spell her own surname. We are not in the business of chasing memes."

A low murmur of agreement. Several proxies had resorted to doom scrolling on their phones.

Vincent stood, chair scraping the stone, and let fly the most withering smile in his repertoire. "Why don't you admit you'd rather paper the cracks and hope the walls don't fall until after you retire? Carmine doesn't care about your decorum. He's not trying to finesse his way back in. We barely contained the Cloak Woman and Bartholemew. He's writing the ending as we speak. I'm not sure you comprehend the gravity of the situation."

The councilwoman with the anvil chin bristled. "You're out of line, Lupo."

"I'm out of patience."

Blackthorn rapped the desk. "Sit down or we will seat you. Permanently."

Vincent sat, but not before muttering, "Maybe we'll submit the apocalypse in triplicate next time."

The proxies were now openly giggling.

Ren's Mark pulsed again, a hot-and-cold tingle that ran up her shoulder and down into her fingers. It hurt—but not in the way she'd expected. The pain was data: line after line of spectral source code rewriting itself, then stalling, then overwriting again, all on the inside of her skin. She dared a glance at Zara, who hovered over the council's main projector, rolling her eyes so hard it was a miracle the afterimage didn't burn into the glass.

Mrs Barley ploughed on, her voice now as brittle as the Council's sense of security. "At minimum, we recommend a full audit of all Carmine-related material held in your archives, active intervention in Moderniser digital feeds, and quarantining of any infected personnel—Council included."

This got Blackthorn's attention. "Are you suggesting the Council itself is compromised?"

Mrs Barley met his gaze. "If Carmine is editing from the root, no one is immune."

A silence more absolute than any declaration of war.

Vincent watched as the elders exchanged the sort of micro-expressions that would have started civil wars in other, more honest centuries. Eventually, Blackthorn signalled a scribe, who stamped the page in front of him with a wet, echoing thunk.

"Your recommendations are noted. However, Council will not cede authority to phantom hypotheses and dissident rumour. The chain of command remains. You will continue surveillance of Moderniser cells, and if there is so much as a whisper of prophecy outside your control, you will report it. Failure to do so will result in—"

"Erasure?" Vincent offered, baring his fangs, but no one took the bait.

"Expulsion," said Blackthorn, who savoured the word like a long-kept grudge. "If any one of you attempts to escalate without authorisation, the Council will erase not only your memory, but your entire contribution to the historical record."

Zara's laughter, which started as a crackle, built to a full poltergeist cackle. "Good luck with that," she said, knowing full well they wouldn't hear her.

Ren, already sweating, wondered if the Mark was trying to warn her or just entertain itself at her expense.

Mrs Barley folded the dossier, sliding it into her bag with the precise resignation of someone who had lost an argument but would not, under any circumstances, admit it. "Understood, Elder Blackthorn."

"Session adjourned," Blackthorn announced, but in the echo of his words you could almost hear the finality of an executioner's axe.

The lights dimmed further as the Council filed out, leaving the three of them to gather their evidence and dignity in the vacuum. The scribe, a waxy wraith in a suit that screamed "adjunct," handed Mrs Barley a stamped and countersigned summary, then left without a word.

Vincent was already halfway to the exit, but Mrs Barley stopped him with a hand on his sleeve. "Don't. They want you to break protocol."

He glared, then relaxed. "You're right."

Ren trailed after them, rubbing her arm and already dreading the next time she had to let the Mark out for air.

Only Zara lingered, drifting along the ceiling with a smile that could have launched a thousand plagues. "Let them think they've won," she whispered, and the sound vibrated in the stone. "They're the ones writing themselves out."

She vanished through the wall, leaving the Council's legacy to rot in the dark.

The others followed, moving as one: Mrs Barley with her silent resolve, Vincent trailing sarcasm like a bad perfume, and Ren, who was almost ready to believe that the prophecy was about her, after all.

The antechamber was pure Council: underheated, underlit, and furnished with seating designed to remind even the unembodied of their corporeal liabilities. A single fluorescent tube buzzed like a trapped horsefly. At the far end, a scribe hunched over a podium the way a barnacle clings to the hull of a ship about to be scuttled. He wore gloves, possibly for the tactile pleasure of rubber on paper, or possibly just to avoid contact with the living.

Vincent, Ren, and Mrs Barley filed in, only to find Zara already lounging in a corner, her face pressed through the wall to watch the corridor beyond. She mouthed a silent countdown as the scribe reached for the first page, then slammed the Council stamp with a force that made the table vibrate and the fluorescent light flicker in sympathy.

He did not look up as he began to read. "You are assigned to surveillance detail Parliament, Commons Chamber. Principal: Member of Parliament Edward Greaves. Affiliation: Unaligned, but with history of Moderniser contact. Purpose: Monitor for viral event, potential Carmine signature. Duration: Until incident is neutralised or superseded by greater threat."

He passed the page to Mrs Barley, who accepted it with the grave delicacy of someone handling a bomb or a birth certificate.

Ren glanced at Vincent. "They want us to watch the Houses of Parliament?"

The scribe continued, each word soaked in resentment. "Should event threshold be reached, you will escalate to the attached contact. No unauthorised action. No media leaks. No use of unlicensed psychic implements within the Palace grounds."

He handed over a second page, which Mrs Barley perused,

then handed to Ren. Vincent didn't bother to take his copy, instead pulling a cigarette from inside his jacket and lighting up despite the clearly posted signage. The scribe's eye twitched, but otherwise showed no signs of mortal distress.

Mrs Barley skimmed the instructions, lips thinning. "It's a trap," she said, soft enough for only the living to hear. "They want us to fail. Or to succeed so publicly that they can't avoid a cull."

Vincent exhaled, filling the air with Council-approved carcinogen. "It's always a trap. The only variable is how many witnesses they want for the show trial."

Ren ran a finger over her Mark, now as warm as a fever. "You think Carmine's aiming for Parliament?"

Vincent's eyes sparkled, but only with the promise of a migraine. "If you were writing a narrative singularity, wouldn't you go straight for the seat of government? Instant global coverage. Plus, it's crawling with people who never listen."

Zara shimmered into visibility beside them, her outline catching the flicker of the fluorescent and turning it into a kind of halo. "Democracy," she mused, "just another draft with too many editors." She hovered above the scribe, mouthing the words along with him as he droned through the last of the protocol.

Mrs Barley squared her shoulders. "We proceed. We watch. We document. Every assignment adds data."

She slipped the pages into her satchel, then stood with the posture of someone determined to drag sense out of chaos, even if it killed her.

The scribe, having completed his reading, looked up for the first time. His eyes were not so much dead as out on long-term loan. "Exit is that way," he said, gesturing to a door marked EXIT in letters that glowed red and suspiciously sticky.

They shuffled through, the door closing behind them with the soft, hydraulic finality of a meat locker.

The corridor beyond led to the Council's main vestibule: two storeys of bare stone and zero history, just the way they liked it. Ren blinked in the sudden cold, then said, "What if we're right? What if the next patch isn't just a livestream, but something bigger?"

Vincent tucked his hands into his pockets and walked, head bowed, voice so low it was barely audible over the echo. "Then Parliament gets its money's worth."

Mrs Barley strode ahead, already diagramming the next move in her mind. "We need eyes on the Member of Parliament for South Basildon and East Thurrock. Zara, you're our inside line for anything the Council can't or won't see."

Zara, for once, looked almost nervous. "I don't do politics," she said, trailing behind them like an uncertain weather front.

"Neither does Parliament," Vincent replied, not breaking stride.

They reached the main doors, heavy oak with a handle worn smooth by centuries of dread. Vincent paused, hand resting on the latch, and looked back at the others.

"You ready?" he asked, but it wasn't really a question.

Mrs Barley nodded. Ren shrugged, the movement so small it could have been mistaken for a shiver.

Zara gave the corridor one last glance, then faded until only her voice remained, soft and seditious. "It's all narrative now," she said. "Just hope you're the one writing it."

Vincent pushed open the doors, and together they stepped

into the London night, where the only thing colder than the wind was the certainty that the next act was already being drafted.

Behind them, the Council's scribe filed away their fate, and in a locked office, Elder Blackthorn began his own preparations for the final cut.

The city hummed with rumours and threat, and above it all, the prophecy waited, ready to propagate at Parliament's first convenience.

TEN

Parliament Square, as it turned out, was the only place in London where the pigeons were outnumbered by police, and the cold was not a function of weather, but of architecture. Vincent arrived first, as usual, having gamed out the logistics of the Jubilee line to guarantee he wouldn't be caught out in the open when the sun rose, and to give himself five minutes alone with the view. He leaned against a frost-rimed column that looked like it had seen at least three revolutions and a televised beheading, hands stuffed into his overcoat pockets, expression tuned to "recently exhumed." The wind off the Thames was bitter enough to strip the enamel from your teeth, and the flags atop Westminster Abbey were at half-mast, though for what or whom, no one could say.

Ren appeared next, bundled in a puffa jacket that made her look faintly larval, eyes wide as she took in the gothic sprawl of Parliament awash in the first pale light of dawn. She walked with the half-stumble of someone who had yet to accept that being awake at this hour was not, in fact, a crime. Her notebook and council-issue clipboard were clamped to her chest with the force of a seatbelt in a crash. She paused at the foot of the statue garden, glancing around with a nervousness that suggested she expected snipers or, worse, interviewers.

Vincent watched her approach and, resisting the urge to call her out, settled for a dry, "You get lost, or are you still orienting by pub density?"

Ren didn't dignify this with a reply. She looked up, scanned the stone faces of a dozen dead statesmen, and muttered, "I thought it'd be bigger."

"It's not the size," Vincent said. "It's the number of padded expenses claims per square foot."

The effect of this line was somewhat diminished by the arrival of Mrs Barley, who strode in from the direction of Lambeth as if she'd power-walked across the bridge just to spite the concept of public transport. She wore a woollen skirt suit in charcoal, white gloves, and a hat with a brim engineered for maximum intimidation. The satchel at her side was bulging with the day's required apparatus, and she greeted the others with a nod that could have been mistaken for affection, if you'd never met her before.

Without a word, she scanned the benches, found the only one free of wet chewing gum and pigeon detritus, and set up shop with the precision of a quartermaster preparing for a siege. Within moments, she'd unpacked three clipboards (pre-filled with Council forms, in triplicate), a set of fake Channel 4 lanyards, and a tartan thermos of tea so potent it could have revived Cromwell. She lined these up along the bench, then gestured for Vincent and Ren to approach.

Vincent sauntered over. Ren followed, nose already running from the cold, eyes watering either from wind or existential horror.

"Operational cover is 'political correspondents,'" Mrs Barley announced. "I have prepared briefing notes for each of us. If challenged, we are credentialed with Channel 4."

Vincent eyed the lanyard. "Couldn't get Sky?"

"They're under investigation," Mrs Barley replied, not missing a beat. She poured three cups of tea, passed them round, then produced a packet of lemon biscuits from her satchel's depths.

Ren, who hadn't spoken since arrival, said, "Are we supposed to be watching or infiltrating?"

Mrs Barley sipped her tea, then set it down. "Both. Greaves is scheduled for a 'policy speech' at ten-fifteen. Until then, we observe, document, and do not engage."

Vincent's lip curled. "Greaves is a coat-hanger with teeth. Even if he's bitten, he's boring."

Mrs Barley raised a brow. "Boring is ideal. Boring does not get us recalled to Council."

Ren flipped through her briefing packet. "He's got a history of... what is this... 'youth outreach'? Is that code?"

"Not code," Vincent said. "Just a different flavour of predation."

There was a sudden, sharp drop in temperature, and for a split second the world went two shades bluer. Zara flickered into being behind the bench, her ghostly outline so faint it barely registered in daylight. She seemed to prefer it that way: her presence was less "haunting" and more "corporate espi-onage." She slid between the pillars, skirt trailing in the wind, and regarded the group with the hollow patience of a Power-Point in limbo.

Vincent didn't turn, just raised his cup in mock salute. "You're late."

Zara ignored this. "Greaves's handler is on site. Suited, cheap shoes, stinks of Eton and dry rot. He's already done three laps."

Mrs Barley nodded. "I have eyes on him. Vincent, stay in the doorway. Ren, focus on ingress routes. I will monitor crowd movement from here."

Vincent drained his tea in a single, chemical burn of a gulp, then stalked off toward cover, shoulders hunched, and steps muffled by the wind. Ren watched him go, then looked at Mrs Barley.

"Is he always like this?" she asked, voice so low it barely cleared the rim of her cup.

Mrs Barley tidied the biscuits back into the tin and set her clipboard on her knees. "Only when the world is ending."

Ren hesitated, then took her post at the edge of the statue garden, scanning the tourists and early morning commuters for anyone who looked like they'd rather be eating a neck than a bacon bap. For a while, nothing happened except the slow rotation of the traffic and the occasional shout from the far side of the square, where a protest was already assembling. The banners were homemade, the slogans unintentionally hilarious: "BRING BACK GOOD OLD PARLIAMENT," "LESS TAX MORE SNACKS," and a personal favourite, "HANG THE DJ."

From time to time, Zara flickered in and out of vision, always just outside of focus, never standing still long enough for a photograph. Occasionally she'd lean close to Mrs Barley's ear and whisper a line of pure poison, which Mrs Barley would then note in her log as if it were the weather report.

At precisely 09:47, a government car nosed its way onto the square, flanked by two security vans and a media scrum so dense it might have been grown in a lab. Greaves, a man who looked exactly like his tabloid caricature—mid-forties, hair the colour of recycled printer paper, suit so shiny it could signal aircraft—stepped out and did the necessary waves. His teeth were blinding, his eyes, less so.

Vincent reappeared in the shadow of the members' entrance, at the edge of the scrum, arms folded. He was close enough to be seen but not, crucially, close enough to attract the attention of security. He shot a look at Mrs Barley and mouthed, "Nothing," then faded back into the flow of bystanders.

Ren, emboldened by the lack of disaster, started taking actual notes, recording who approached Greaves, who shook his hand, and who left fingerprints on the bonnet of the car. She noticed two Modernisers among the crowd—easily identified by the ring lights and the compulsion to pose for every passing iPhone. One was already live-streaming, grinning for an audience of thousands as she tried to catch Greaves in a viral moment.

Zara materialised beside Ren, just long enough to say, "If he has a tell, it's in the left hand. Always fiddling. Means he's lying."

Ren nearly dropped her clipboard. "You're a ghost, why do you care about tells?"

"Dead or not, nobody likes being conned," Zara said, and

then she was gone, leaving only the scent of ozone and ancient dust.

The hour ticked over. The crowd doubled. The protestors, now emboldened by the cameras, began to chant, though the effect was less "people's movement" and more "charity fun run gone wrong." Mrs Barley watched it all, marking up her forms with a speed and accuracy that would have earned a medal in the pre-digital Olympics.

As ten-fifteen approached, Greaves's team set up a temporary lectern beneath the stone lions, and the MP did a slow, calculated sweep of the square before ascending. There was no sign of panic, no sign of vampiric anomaly, just the cold logic of a man who had prepped every moment and was now determined to survive it.

Vincent, standing in the shadow of a column, whispered into his lapel mic: "Showtime. But don't blink."

Mrs Barley, already writing, murmured, "Eyes open, voices off."

The square hushed. Greaves began to speak, voice clear and rehearsed, every syllable calibrated for the cameras and, presumably, the eventual news cycle.

For a moment, nothing happened.

But even in that moment, Vincent felt the undercurrent—something old, something hungry, shifting beneath the surface of the morning. He glanced up, caught Ren's eye, and for once, said nothing. There was no need. The story, as always, was about to write itself.

If Parliament Square had resembled an anthill before, by ten past ten it had mutated into the command centre for an unannounced coup. The traffic islands were barricaded with news vans, each sporting a different logo and a drone operator with more hair gel than sense. Cables snaked across the pavement, converging in a tangle of temporary fencing and nervous PR staff. The "public" area overflowed with a mixture of paid agitators, tourists in high-vis jackets and matching backpacks, and influencers who hadn't bothered with credentials, convinced that their ring lights were passport enough.

Vincent watched from the shade of the doorway, unamused by either the spectacle or the bone ache crawling up his arm. He surveyed the growing mob with the detachment of a war historian, or perhaps a man who had lost more than one city to public hysteria. The cold had sharpened his senses and flattened his mood; he lit a cigarette with the air of a condemned man and watched the smoke drift toward the first ranks of the crowd.

Ren had stationed herself at the base of the steps, clipboard balanced on her knee, biro dancing as she scribbled observations. She had abandoned any pretence of casual note-taking; her eyes flicked constantly between the aides scuttling along the inner corridor of Westminster and the Modernisers out on the square, who seemed to multiply every time she looked up. They wore the usual: distressed velvet, hashtag-branded scarves, and the kind of fangs that came in six-packs at Poundland. Two were already live-streaming, narrating the buildup with a confidence that could only have come from being retweeted by the right account.

At the back of the square, a minor brawl broke out between rival podcasters, the air filling with shrieks and the wet sound of coffee hitting a protestor's jacket. Vincent snorted, half with contempt, half with a nostalgia he didn't dare examine.

Mrs Barley, impervious to chaos, stood at her post near the security cordon, the only civilian on the inside of the velvet rope who looked like she'd be more at home running the operation than observing it. She tracked Greaves's movements through a pair of compact binoculars, her lips moving in a silent litany as she logged each deviation from the advance schedule. The thermos was gone, replaced by a discreet earpiece and a second clipboard, this one sheathed in a plastic wallet stamped "COUNCIL: LEVEL FOUR."

Zara appeared now and again in the eddies of the crowd, but each time she did, the digital signal spiked, causing every phone within five metres to glitch for a heartbeat and every live stream to freeze on a shot of her spectral face. The influencers chalked it up to "government Wi-Fi sabotage" and doubled down, waving their phones at the podium as if they could exorcise the ghost by giving her better lighting.

On the upper steps, the main event began to coalesce. Greaves's team unfurled a Union Jack banner, the corners weighted with sandbags in case of wind or opportunistic protestors. Greaves himself paced behind the lectern, notes clutched in one hand, the other flicking compulsively at his cuff-links. His aides buzzed around him like midges, checking their watches and muttering in Bluetooth.

Ren focused on the aides, jotting names and possible affiliations. She watched as one slipped away to the side, pausing to take a phone call behind a decorative yew. Ren wrote "call at 10:13—too long for a quick hello to a boyfriend, not enough for a deal" in the margin of her form, then made a sketch of the woman's face, which was sharp-featured and somehow both familiar and instantly forgettable.

Vincent's voice crackled in her earpiece, low and bone-dry. "Our man's left cuff is loaded. Either a glamoured wound or a comms unit. Either way, he's hiding something."

"Copy," Ren whispered, ducking as a pair of council workers trundled past with a trolley full of complementary biscuits. "The aide in green is on the move again. She's talking to the Moderniser cluster at the North Gate."

Mrs Barley's response was immediate, clipped, and final: "Stay clear. They're rolling in outside contractors."

Ren winced as a sudden, hot prickling surged under her sleeve. For a moment, the world blurred at the edge, and all she could focus on was the sickly pulse of the Editor's Mark, now livid with its own private fever. She gritted her teeth, eyes watering, and pressed her arm to her side, fingers digging into the flesh just above her wrist. Through the fabric, she could feel the Mark crawling, reshaping itself, as if it were trying to reach out and write itself onto the air.

She risked a glance at Vincent, who was watching her, eyes narrowed. He gave the tiniest shake of his head—*Don't make a scene*, or *Don't let them see*—but she couldn't tell which.

The hum of the square reached a crescendo as the cameras swung round to the podium. Greaves stepped forward, adjusted his tie, and tapped the microphone. A dozen news crews, three radio stations, and at least one covert Council relay caught every syllable as he began:

"Good morning. Today, we gather not only as citizens, but as stewards of the future—"

Vincent rolled his eyes. "You'd think with all their history,

Parliament would've learned to spot a coup before it happened."

Mrs Barley ignored him, focused on the speech. She scanned the crowd, eyes ticking off every Moderniser, every "concerned citizen" whose face wouldn't match their lanyard or passport. She saw them: the plants, the shills, the living proxies that the Council had failed to erase. Each watched the speech with a fanatic's gleam, phones held high, recording every word.

Ren's arm blazed with heat. It was a struggle to keep her hand from shaking as she wrote, the pen carving deep, ragged lines into the page. Each syllable of Greaves's speech seemed to reverberate inside her Mark, as if he were speaking directly to it —or through it.

On the screen of her own phone, which she'd propped discreetly in the margin of her file, the live feed from the Modernisers glitched. For a split second, the video stuttered, then overlaid with a flash of text, just visible enough to read: "HISTORY IS WRITTEN IN BLOOD. PATCH READY."

Ren's breath caught in her throat. She looked up, and for a moment every face in the crowd wore the same glassy, anticipatory expression: a moment before the punchline, or the drop, or the first shot.

Greaves went on, voice rising: "Let us not be divided by the old rhetoric of fear and suspicion—let us embrace the power of shared memory, of collective narrative—"

Vincent muttered into the mic: "That's it. He's primed the payload."

Mrs Barley's response was all ice: "If you're right, we have thirty seconds before it propagates."

Ren, desperate now, pressed her sleeve to her arm. She could feel the Mark throbbing, the edges curling and uncurling, the colour bleeding through the fabric in flickers of blue and green and a hint of red. The pain was less pain now and more a pressure, as if a fist were closing around her forearm from the inside.

The first Moderniser in the crowd began to chant. It was quiet, at first, lost beneath the noise of the square, but it grew—one, then three, then a dozen voices, all repeating the same, perfectly synchronised line:

"Feed the future. Bleed the past."

Vincent saw it happen. He moved, fast and silent, cutting through the back of the crowd toward the Moderniser cluster. He didn't need to check if Mrs Barley or Ren was following; this was not a team sport.

Ren tried to stand, but her knees buckled. The Mark was in command now, her hand scribbling on its own, carving lines she didn't recognise into the edge of her notes. She bit back a scream, managed to stagger into the press of bodies, and let the crowd carry her forward.

On the steps, Greaves's voice was drowned out by the chant. He hesitated, looked up, and in that instant, his eyes changed—not colour, not shape, just a sudden, electric focus, as if he'd been waiting for the feedback loop to complete.

Ren felt the world slide sideways, the ground lurching beneath her. The pain peaked, then shattered into something colder: the Mark split, the segments reconfiguring, and she saw —inside her head, or maybe outside—what the next line of the prophecy would be.

Zara's ghost materialised in the melee, her outline burning

blue in the daylight. She reached for Ren, her voice a high, impossible frequency:

"Don't let it patch you. Hold the draft."

Ren gripped the clipboard with both hands and willed herself not to pass out.

Vincent reached the Moderniser cluster just as the first true anomaly hit. The air twisted, an ozone snap, and every phone in the square exploded in a bloom of white light. The sound was deafening—a million digital feedbacks all howling at once.

Mrs Barley barked a single word into her mic: "Now."

Vincent knew what she meant. He lunged for the lead Moderniser, grabbed her by the collar, and yanked her off her feet. She hissed, baring fangs, but Vincent didn't flinch; he slammed her to the ground, pinned her with a knee, and watched as the rest of her cohort staggered, clutching at their own arms, wrists, and necks.

Ren was in the epicentre. The Mark was on fire, the pain coiling up her shoulder, into her jaw, into her teeth. She felt every syllable of the prophecy etch itself into her bones. The world dissolved into blue, and the only thing that kept her standing was the pressure of bodies all around, all chanting, all infected with the same line of code.

Through the noise, Zara's voice reached her again, softer now:

"It's just a draft. It's not the ending."

Greaves, at the podium, looked out across the chaos. He smiled—an awful, predatory thing—and raised his left hand. For a moment, the world held its breath.

Ren, with the last of her strength, tore the page from her

clipboard and crumpled it in her fist. The Mark flared one final time, then went cold. She collapsed to her knees, gasping, as the chanting faltered, then died.

In the silence that followed, Greaves collected his notes, stepped back from the microphone, and vanished into the building.

Vincent released the Moderniser, who whimpered and lay still. He staggered to his feet, scanned the crowd for Ren, and found her, pale and shaking, but alive.

Mrs Barley met them at the edge of the steps, clipboard clutched so tight her fingers were bone white.

For a long time, no one spoke.

Then, slowly, the crowd began to disperse. The news vans packed up. The influencers, shaken, streamed away in twos and threes, muttering about blackouts and lost footage. The only evidence that anything had happened was the faint, fading echo of the chant, and the blood on Vincent's knuckles.

Zara hovered beside Ren, gaze gentle, almost proud. "You held the line."

Ren managed a shaky smile. "I think I broke the pen."

Vincent, exhausted, took her by the shoulder. "Not just the pen, kid."

Mrs Barley straightened her jacket, checked her watch, and said, "We'll need to file a report."

Vincent rolled his eyes. "Always the paperwork."

But for once, Ren didn't mind. She'd earned the right to write the ending.

They stood together on the steps of Parliament, watching as the city slowly, inevitably, reset itself for the next disaster.

Above them, the sky was still grey, but the cold didn't bite as hard.

For now.

ELEVEN

At the head of the Council chamber hall, Elder Blackthorn—presiding, pontificating, and quite possibly on the cusp of spontaneous combustion—raised his silver-tipped cane and struck the marble floor with a sound like a firing squad in stereo.

"Council will come to order," he boomed, the vowels crisp as hailstones.

Around him, the Council elders arranged themselves in two tiers: the front row of Proper Vampires, each with a different flavour of permafrost for a face; the rear, proxies and clerks, every one of them bred to the task of collective outrage. Several wielded folding fans, which they snapped open and shut in bursts of semaphore that signalled nothing so much as "I wish you were dead, but Council says we mustn't say so."

Blackthorn began the performance by unfurling a copy of *The Times*, the front page screaming: VAMPIRE APOCALYPSE AT PARLIAMENT—MPS DEMAND INQUIRY. The inky headline trembled as he shook the page for emphasis.

"Do you see this?" he demanded, waving it at the accused as if expecting them to burst into flame. "This is what the mortals read at breakfast now. It is your doing."

He fixed Vincent with a gaze that could have sandblasted glass. "Lupo, you have been a plague on this Council for centuries. But this—" he jabbed at the paper, "—this is the worst yet."

Vincent regarded the headline with all the enthusiasm of a condemned man asked to choose his own rope. "If you're upset about the photos, Elder, I agree: not my best angle. Though the wardrobe was inspired."

A hiss ran around the benches, a gust of disapproval so intense the candle flames leaned away. Blackthorn ignored it, turning the page with surgical precision.

"And you, Mrs Barley. You were charged with containment. Instead, we have Modernisers on every broadcast, news drones filming daylight feeding, and Parliament itself—*Parliament*—suggesting a 'Vampire Regulatory Agency.'"

Mrs Barley held his gaze, unsmiling. "Council surveillance notes confirm it was not glamour failure, but a premeditated event. The infection vector was deliberate. This was not a lapse. It was a strike."

"Of course you would say so," Blackthorn sneered. "What is your evidence?"

Mrs Barley produced, with a crispness that verged on violence, a dossier from her satchel. She laid it on the rail, opening to a page marked with at least four warning tabs. "Forensic readings from the aftermath show concentrated prophecy traces, all bearing Carmine's signature. The pattern of escalation is consistent with the recursion outbreaks of—"

The Councilwoman with sharp jawline interrupted with a derisive flutter of fan. "Oh, please. Every time something escapes your coterie, it's 'Carmine's recursion.' Why not blame the weather, or Brexit?"

Mrs Barley did not dignify this with a blink. "Because the weather cannot hijack a Moderniser livestream and inject Carmine's own script into the autocue. Nor can Brexit leave triple-coded spectral sigils in the main chamber of Parliament. Carmine can."

Vincent caught Ren's eye; she looked like she'd just seen someone murder her favourite algorithm. He wanted to squeeze her shoulder, say "we're nearly through this," but suspected it would only draw more attention.

Blackthorn rapped the dais with his cane. "Enough. We do not acknowledge myth, only failures. This was a failure. Worse, it was a spectacular, viral, and above all, public failure." He let the word "public" linger like a dog turd in a bath.

Vincent, never one to miss a cue, piped up. "Perhaps if the Council invested in media training—"

"Silence!" snapped Blackthorn, but he was already scanning the next headline, a tabloid with the cover: UNDEAD MP? GREAVES SEEN WITH 'BLOOD EYES'—SEE PAGE 3 FOR THE SHOCKING PHOTOS.

Mrs Barley spoke before the next wave of accusations. "If I may, Elder—containment is impossible once the viral threshold is passed. Modern media is the vector, not the cause. The prophecy is adapting to exploit the system."

"You are the system," said Blackthorn. "You were meant to be immune."

Ren spoke for the first time, voice cracking like frost. "There is no immunity. The Mark re-writes itself every time someone repeats the phrase. It's already in the memes, in the hashtags. Even Council proxies are quoting it. The recursion's self-propagating."

For a moment, the chamber held its breath. Even the fans ceased their orchestral sniping.

Blackthorn rounded on her, voice gone brittle. "You, the human, presume to instruct this Council?"

Ren met his gaze, not defiant but unblinking, the way only the truly exhausted can manage. "No, Elder. I'm just saying you can't fix a viral prophecy with a press release."

The sharp-chinned Councilwoman hissed, baring a set of canines that would have been more impressive if they hadn't been upstaged by the main event. "What do you propose, then? More hashtags? A podcast?"

Vincent laughed, a brittle sound. "Maybe start by not threatening to erase us every time there's a problem."

This time the Council did not hiss. Instead, a series of glares converged on him so hard he could feel the marrow in his bones try to change its name by deed poll.

Blackthorn leaned forward, eyes gone full lamprey. "Another leak, Lupo, and we will ensure you are erased. Permanently."

Vincent held his ground, though his hand trembled ever so slightly as he extracted a cigarette from behind his ear. "Understood, Elder. But if Carmine's running the show now, you might as well erase the lot of us. The world's already on his script."

Mrs Barley packed up her folder, lips thin. "We await Council's pleasure," she said, knowing full well what came next.

Blackthorn straightened, gavel in hand. "Council will

consider your testimony. Until then, you are on your last warning. You may not speak to the press, Council agents, or, ideally, each other. If you do, we will unmake you in ways that will be studied for generations."

He pounded the gavel, the sound echoing like a mass grave being closed. The torches guttered, and the Council filed out in a flurry of silks and sneers.

For a moment, the trio stood alone in the gloom, the only warmth in the room radiating from Ren's Mark, which was already crawling up her sleeve in a slow, phosphor pulse.

Vincent lit a cigarette with hands that shook just enough to betray how close he was to collapse. "Well," he said, exhaling a plume of blue smoke that snaked toward the vanished Council. "I suppose we're lucky they didn't just have us shot. Or worse: promoted to PR."

Ren managed a weak laugh. Mrs Barley collected her things, then paused, fixing Vincent with a stare equal parts steel and something softer.

"We're not done," she said, voice low. "Not by a long way."

Vincent nodded, cradling the cigarette like it was a blood bag in disguise. "No," he agreed. "We're just the first draft."

They left the chamber together, their shadows long and stitched together by the guttering light, three points of resistance against a history that was determined to rewrite them out.

The Council's vestibule, a hundred feet of damp flagstones and penitential gloom, was empty but for the condemned and the permanently underemployed. Cold torches guttered in iron brackets, their light the sickly green of pond algae and municipal envy. Even the air conspired against comfort; every draft of wind up from the sub-basements reeked of wet limestone and dead optimism.

Ren slumped against the wall beneath a rusted candelabra, breath fogging in the corridor's chill. She rolled up her sleeve to expose the Mark, which now pulsed under her skin with a slow, sullen heartbeat.

Vincent leaned beside her, both of them in the shadow of a vast, pointed arch that made even his frame look malnourished. He shook out another cigarette, then remembered where he was and snapped the pack shut again.

Mrs Barley stood a discrete distance off, jotting notations in a notebook with a silver fountain pen. Even her handwriting looked like it could pass a breathalyser.

Vincent broke the silence first. "So, that went about as well as Council karaoke night."

No one laughed. Ren flexed her arm, watching as the Mark cycled from cobalt to sickly green and back again. "It glowed during the speech," she said, voice cracked. "Every time Greaves repeated the line, it was like—like it was syncing with him. With Carmine, or whoever's behind it."

Vincent studied the Mark, then Ren's face. "You sure it's not just performance anxiety? I hear Parliament has that effect on a lot of people."

Ren managed a snort, but it was all surface. "I'm not scared of MPs. I'm scared of being overwritten by an actual recursive prophecy."

Mrs Barley glanced up from her notes. "It's not just you.

The entire feed is infected. I checked the Council's own press office before we went in. Every site, every news brief—it's in the comments, in the auto-captioning, even the translation layers." She clicked her pen shut with a sound like a switchblade. "They're not trying to solve it. They're trying to bury it."

Vincent tried to shrug, but the movement came out closer to a wince. He fished a hip flask from his coat, unscrewed it, and offered it to Ren.

She eyed the flask. "Is this even legal?"

He grinned. "It's medicinal. For when you've been threatened with comprehensive erasure and can't afford therapy."

She took a gulp. The taste was hot and medicinal, but it helped. "Thanks."

Vincent drank, then passed the flask to Mrs Barley, who ignored it with the efficiency of someone who had seen a thousand such gestures and never once been moved to join in.

Down the corridor, a passing vampire—one of Blackthorn's junior enforcers—glided by carrying a plate of what looked like roasted marrow bones and something that stank of raw garlic. The scent hit Vincent mid-sentence. He reeled, clutching his wrist, which still bore the red-raw imprint of yesterday's burn.

Ren caught the wince. "You're still not healed?"

He looked at the burn, then at her, forcing a smile that showed too much tooth. "You should see the other guy."

Mrs Barley interrupted, snapping her notebook closed. "If you're done with the comedy hour, we should move. Council's not above surveillance, even out here."

Vincent nodded, the hunger in his eyes suddenly more pronounced. "They never did trust the dead not to gossip." He turned to Ren, voice low and urgent. "How bad is it? Really."

She hesitated, then rolled her sleeve all the way up. The Mark had spread, creeping up her arm in filaments that shimmered with every pulse. "I don't know. Feels like it's running hot, like it wants to break containment. If I think about the prophecy, it—" She broke off, eyes wide. "It's not just in me, Vincent. I can hear it in other people. Echoing. Like we're all on the same network."

Mrs Barley's face twitched, just once. "You're a node. Not the payload, but a relay."

Ren nodded. "And Carmine's running the updates."

A gust of cold air swept the corridor, and with it, Zara appeared—half-solid, half-static, the light bending and warping around her in bands of cerulean and ultraviolet. She hovered a foot above the ground, her feet phasing in and out of the flagstone as if daring anyone to tell her not to.

"Well," she said, voice carrying a modulated reverb, "that could have gone worse. At least they didn't drag out the oubliette." She drifted closer, examining Ren's Mark with the avid curiosity of a research biologist confronted by a talking tumour. "That's new," she said. "I like the branching. Very 'early internet'."

Vincent gritted his teeth, hands balled into fists. "Carmine's not going away just because the Council files it under 'embarrassment.'"

"Of course not," said Zara. "He never played by committee rules. He likes to skip to the end, overwrite the last page." She made a gesture that was either a wave or a rude gesture, then regarded the trio with something like approval. "You lot are the only ones who might get ahead of him."

Ren looked up, Mark still glowing. "How? They'll erase us if we go off-script."

Zara grinned, blue fire at the corners of her mouth. "Then don't get caught."

Mrs Barley tucked her notebook away, face set in a line. "We need to isolate the Mark. Find out how it's propagating. If we can disrupt the network, we might be able to slow Carmine's updates."

Vincent nodded, the motion barely controlled. "And if not?"

Mrs Barley smiled, the first time Vincent had seen her do so without irony. "Then we give him a story he can't rewrite."

A beat. Then, quietly, Vincent said, "So we're on our own."

"Always have been," said Zara. "It's what makes you dangerous."

The four of them stood in the corridor, the air thick with the stench of candle wax, and impending doom. For a moment, there was nothing but the pulse of the Mark, the flicker of torchlight, and the shared, unspoken knowledge that the Council would never save them.

TWELVE

The kitchen, if one were charitable enough to call it that, had survived at least four major metaphysical incidents, two fridge fires, and a summer in which Zara attempted to ferment her own kombucha using nothing but raw sugar and the psychic detritus of the British Library's rare books collection. By dusk it had reverted to its default state: ancient linoleum, a sink full of relics and regrets, and the kind of counterspace that could only be described as "not fit for purpose" by anyone with a healthy sense of self-preservation.

Moonlight—anaemic, apologetic, and wholly unequal to the task of banishing the day's residue—spilled through a curtain that had once been blue but now mostly broadcast an impression of mildew. It limned the dust motes in the air, illuminated the uncollected recycling, and finally, as if shamed by its own persistence, fell onto Ren, who had stationed herself between the worktop and the oven in a defensive crouch perfected by millions of over-caffeinated Londoners before her.

She was making breakfast at eight p.m. Not a metaphorical breakfast, but the real, honest kind that involved eggs, toast, and a packet of garlic cloves she'd found buried behind a sack of lentils in the cupboard. The eggs hissed in the pan, edges going lace-brown. Ren fished a clove from the mesh netting and whacked it with the flat of her knife, sending shards and juice in every direction.

Vincent sat slouched at the corner of the table, watching the proceedings through eyelids at half-mast. He looked as if he'd been poured into his chair sometime in the previous century and no one had gotten around to extracting him. His skin had the waxen pallor of a week spent punching above his existential weight class, and his knuckles—bandaged, barely—rested on a mug of blood-spiked coffee that he'd been using as both hand-warmer and pretext for not speaking.

Mrs Barley stood in the doorway, posture perfectly perpendicular to the lino, not so much present as observing at a molecular level. She had a note pad out, its cover already scarred with fresh ballpoint furrows, and she was writing in the cramped, assassin's hand of someone who planned to archive the world's failings one margin note at a time.

The smell of garlic and burnt egg hit first. The second smell —a sharp, chemical flare—came a heartbeat later, as a stray piece of crushed garlic ricocheted off the knife blade, skidded across the Formica, and tumbled directly onto the back of Vincent's hand.

He did not react in the expected way. No hiss, no melodramatic recoil, no lecture about the sanctity of allium-free kitchens. Instead, the spot where the garlic touched his skin sizzled. Truly sizzled, as if someone had turned on a miniature sun beneath his epidermis. The skin went a raw, alarming red, then puckered and lifted in a half-moon blister, juice boiling on the surface. For a moment, he just stared at it, eyes uncomprehending. Then, in the kind of slow-motion horror usually reserved for dashcam footage, he drew his hand back, flexed the fingers, and made a sound that was somewhere between a gasp and a snarl.

Ren heard the noise and turned, still holding the knife. "Shit. Sorry—didn't think you were that close."

Vincent tried to smooth the event into normalcy. "It's fine. Breakfast is meant to be hazardous. Builds character."

Ren watched as he dabbed the wound with a napkin, which promptly stuck to the blister in a way that made both of them wince. "No, that's not—" She took a step closer, peering at the site of injury. "It shouldn't do that. You've never—"

"Everything's a first time," he said, and peeled the napkin away with the stoicism of a man who had seen his share of worse and wasn't about to let a kitchen accident be the thing that broke him.

Mrs Barley, from the threshold: "Was that an involuntary reflex, or were you attempting to suppress it?"

Vincent didn't bother looking at her. "Both."

She nodded once, made a note. "Degree of reaction?"

He looked at the burn again. It was already seeping, the edges angry and white. "Eight out of ten. Nine if you're into the finer points of sadism."

Ren set the knife down and crossed her arms, eyeing Vincent with the same appraisal she reserved for borrowed laptops that returned from the field with mystery dents. "That wasn't normal."

Vincent flashed a grin that might have convinced a less invested observer. "Nothing about me is."

But Ren didn't buy it. She reached for the garlic, looked at it, then at the burn, then at Vincent. "It's getting worse, isn't it?"

He shrugged. "Depends how you feel about breakfast theatre."

The tension was not theatrical. If anything, it had the leaden, room-collapsing quality of a disaster in slow motion. The burn was already spreading, spiderwebbing out from the point of contact. Vincent pressed the cold mug to it, watched the pinkish condensation bead on the porcelain, and decided he'd rather it scalded than risk another comment from the peanut gallery.

Mrs Barley turned a page in her pad. "The garlic reaction indicates an acceleration. Vampiric sensitivities usually plateau at conversion, but this appears to be a second-order mutation. Possibly related to the recursion vector."

Vincent bared his teeth. "Thank you, Dr House. Always wanted to be a case study."

Ren shook her head, voice softening. "You're not a case study. But you need to take this seriously. If it's mutating—"

He cut her off. "If it's mutating, there's nothing to do but ride it out. You think the Council's going to help?" He looked at Mrs Barley, then back at Ren. "They've already marked me as defective. Soon as I go critical, they'll black-bag the lot and send what's left to R&D."

Mrs Barley did not deny this. "Council containment is more likely than assistance, yes. But early documentation may provide mitigation strategies."

Vincent smirked. "Glad to be of service."

The kitchen fell silent, save for the slow death of the eggs in the pan. Ren, unwilling to let it drop, reached for the first aid kit stashed behind the toaster and offered Vincent the tube of burn ointment. He took it with a small nod, dabbed it on with exaggerated care, then rolled down his sleeve to cover the site.

"Breakfast?" Ren asked, voice tentative.

"Appetite's gone," Vincent said, but he didn't leave the table. Instead, he picked up the cold mug, cradling it like it might anchor him to the present, and stared out of the window at the night beyond.

Mrs Barley capped her pen, tore the sheet from her pad, and tucked it into her bag. "Observation: the progression rate is increasing. You may wish to consider palliative measures."

Vincent didn't look up. "Like what? More garlic, or something with a bit more character?"

Mrs Barley met his sarcasm with absolute neutrality. "Limit exposure to triggers. Document changes. Notify us if you experience further deviation from baseline."

He laughed, a hollow sound. "If I make it to lunch, I'll send a memo."

Ren tried to salvage the eggs, but the smell of garlic and burnt vampire skin had fused into a single, inescapable presence. She scooped the mess straight into the bin, poured a glass of water, and slid into the seat opposite. Her eyes never left his hand.

Mrs Barley lingered in the doorway, gaze flickering between the two. For the first time, she seemed at a loss for what to document. "I'll be in the archive," she said, and left without waiting for a reply.

The silence returned, heavier this time. Vincent poked at

his hand, then at the burn. He didn't say anything, but Ren could read the equation: the world was closing in, and even the constants were shifting underfoot.

"Let me know if you need help," she said, voice almost inaudible.

Vincent nodded, and for a moment, the only sound was the slow ticking of the kitchen clock, and the chemical crackle of garlic juice eating into his skin.

Outside, the city slept on, indifferent to the fact that one of its oldest monsters was now in a race with his own immune system.

It was, in its way, the perfect metaphor for the night ahead.

The common area of Zara's (now Ren's) flat had always aspired to a kind of neglect that felt intentional. At this hour, it had achieved something grander—a version of darkness that wasn't total, but preferred to linger at the edges and seep into the centre only when absolutely necessary. The blinds were three-quarters closed, city light leaking through in pale, sodium stripes. Everything looked jaundiced, as if the building's very bones were decaying under the weight of London's collective fatigue.

Vincent still occupied the ancient, sagging armchair by the window, a silhouette framed against the dull glow of streetlamps and the intermittent blue of police lights chasing themselves up Holloway Road. He sat perfectly still, one hand curled around the armrest, the other resting on his knee, fingers drumming a rhythm at war with the pulse in his neck.

His jaw hurt. Not the kind of pain that responded to whiskey or willpower, but a deeper, grinding pressure, as if the bones themselves had begun to rebel. The fangs were the worst —nails of ice, pressing from the inside, refusing to retract even when he willed them up with all the authority of seven centuries of bad habits. He pressed his tongue to the roof of his mouth, hoping to soothe the ache, but it only made things worse. The taste was off: bitter and metal, the hint of old pennies and new pain.

Hunger rode shotgun, as always, but now it had company. The need for blood was no longer a manageable inconvenience; it was the ghost of a migraine, lurking just outside the field of vision, waiting for any lapse in control. He tried to ignore it. He tried to pretend he could still run on adrenaline, or spite, or whatever else had gotten him through the last seven centuries.

It was no use.

He reached into the cooler bag that lived beneath the armchair, fished out a medical blood pouch, and held it up to the lamp. The contents sloshed a dull, uncompromising red. It was the kind of hospital-grade blood that arrived via dodgy back channels and was meant for emergencies and special occasions, not for lunch. But Vincent was way past that distinction. He tore the tab open with a snap, pressed the plastic nozzle to his lips, and drank.

It tasted like hospital, like the air in a waiting room at three a.m., like someone else's bad memories poured into a carrier bag and left to ripen. It didn't matter. He drank deep, cold blood sliding down his throat, and for a moment, the world steadied on its axis. The hunger, once a roaring in his head, dialled back to a mere whine.

He let the empty bag drop to the floor, wiped his mouth with the back of his sleeve. He immediately felt a little more like Vincent, a little less monstrous. But only a little.

He heard the soft tread of footsteps before he smelled her— Ren, back from wherever she'd been stashing the detritus of her own breakdown. She stepped into the living room with the reluctance of someone who'd opened a lot of doors and found nothing good on the other side.

She froze when she saw him, the blood bag discarded on the floor, the evidence of his failure smeared on his chin.

"Didn't mean to interrupt," she said, voice brittle but steady.

Vincent shook his head, tried for a joke, but nothing came. He settled for a non-committal grunt and stared at the pattern the city lights made on the glass.

Ren lingered in the doorway, arms crossed tight, body language closed for business. "Mrs Barley's still in the archive," she said, as if it mattered. "Probably planning your funeral. Or your next career move."

Vincent offered the ghost of a smile. "There's no pension in this line of work."

She didn't move. "You okay?"

He looked at the empty bag, then at his own hand, which trembled with a fine, embarrassing shake. "Define 'okay'."

Ren took a step into the room, the silence between them stretching so thin it could have sliced skin. "You're changing," she said. No accusation, just fact.

Vincent turned, baring his teeth before he realised what he was doing. The snarl was animal, not his usual brand of performance. It filled the air for a second, made the shadows on the walls jump. He snapped his mouth shut, horror and shame crashing through him in the same instant.

He looked away, voice flat. "Congratulations. You've cracked the obvious."

Ren said nothing, just watched him with the eyes of someone who had spent her whole life studying systems right up until the moment they collapsed.

Vincent licked his lips, tasting the blood, the hunger, and something underneath—something cold and viral, the echo of Carmine's prophecy worming its way deeper. He wondered if he could ever dig it out, or if this was simply what he was now.

He tried to rise, but the room spun. He steadied himself on the armrest, knuckles white, vision tunnelling. "If I lose it," he said, forcing the words past his tongue, "you know what to do."

Ren's face hardened. "Don't make me."

He laughed, short and ugly. "You won't have to. If it gets bad, I'll walk out myself. Leave a note."

She crossed to him, slow but certain, and set her hand on his shoulder. The touch was light, almost careful. "You're not alone, Vincent."

He wanted to believe her. He really did. But he knew how these things went—the man sitting in the chair was already gone, replaced by a ghost stitched together with regret and borrowed time.

The city kept on, indifferent, the sodium lights washing everything in a colourless hope. Ren stood with him, not speaking, not moving, until the trembling in his hands stilled and the ache in his jaw faded to a tolerable throb.

They stayed there, silent, both pretending they had more time than they did.

THIRTEEN

Ren's flat was never warm, not even with the central heating on full, and tonight it was colder than a solicitor's handshake. The rain outside had ambitions, hurling itself at the windows in great arterial spurts that made even the roaches hesitate at the threshold. The walls were the kind of eggshell yellow that only ever reminded you of institutional cooking, and strips of paint hung from the skirting like dead skin. On the mantelpiece, a clutter of old receipts, Council mail, and battered paperbacks leaned at suicidal angles, as if holding each other up only by the threat of mutual embarrassment.

Vincent stood by the window, pretending to look at the street, actually watching the glass. He'd stopped casting a proper reflection centuries ago, but now it was worse: he could see a vague dark shape, half his own, half someone else's, and the movement inside it was never quite in time with his own.

He'd forgotten Ren was still in the room, until she was close enough to jab him in the spine with the end of a biro. Not a hard jab, more a warning shot. Her voice followed, pitched to the perfect register for waking the dead (or just making them wish for that luxury).

"Don't move," she said. "I need a good look at you."

Vincent didn't turn. "You planning to sketch my profile for posterity?"

She jabbed again, this time a little higher. "You smell like hospital disinfectant and someone else's blood. You're not even pretending anymore, are you?"

"I could shower," Vincent said, "but I think the pipes are on strike."

Ren circled him, staying just outside arm's reach, as if he might try something feral. Her eyes travelled from his face to his hands, where the garlic burn had flowered into a puckered, ugly white blister.

"Show me," she said.

Vincent hesitated a fraction too long, which was all the invitation she needed. She grabbed his wrist and yanked his sleeve up, exposing the angry ring of dead skin. Her lips tightened, not in sympathy but in that grim I-told-you-so way that only the truly aggrieved can muster.

"It's nothing," Vincent replied, pulling his arm away. "Just—"

Ren cut him off, dropping his hand like it was the very thing it was: toxic. "Nothing is for mortals. That is... advanced."

Vincent reached for the sideboard, fumbled in the detritus for a glass, and poured himself a slug of wine. He'd long ago stopped pretending it was for the taste.

"You're overreacting," he said, but it came out without conviction.

Ren plucked a battered hardback from the sofa, using it as a makeshift shield. "You're not just drinking more," she said. "You're becoming more."

He laughed, sharp and thin. "What, moodier? Older? Hungrier? That's just middle age, kid."

Ren advanced, keeping the book between them like a crucifix. "You're not funny, Vincent. You never really were. And you're not fooling anyone."

He drained the glass and set it down, face suddenly very tired. "What do you want me to say? That the Mark's fucking with my head? That when I look in the mirror, I see something else staring back?"

Ren didn't answer. She let the silence do its work.

Vincent cracked first. "Fine. Yes. I'm changing. Maybe not in the way the Council thought, but—"

"You think?" Ren spat, voice rising. "You're not just a hazard to yourself, you're a hazard, period. I've seen how you look at people in crowds now. You do the calculation, every time. Who's weak. Who'd go missing. Who'd be easy to drag into a stairwell and drain."

That stung, and she knew it.

He tried to muster some sarcasm, but the old magic wasn't there. "Congratulations, you're observant."

Ren leaned in, close enough for him to see the cracks in her composure. "Stop pretending this is funny," she said. "I need to know if you're dangerous—to me."

He recoiled as if struck, mouth open, then closed again. A

full second passed. Then another. The air thickened with all the things neither of them could say, until it was a wonder the rain didn't break through the window out of sheer embarrassment.

Vincent looked down at his hands, flexed them as if seeing the bones underneath for the first time. "I'm not," he said, but even he didn't believe it.

Ren dropped the book onto the coffee table with a thump that sent a small flock of dust motes into the air. "That's not good enough," she said. "Because if you can't promise me, I have to go. I have people who'd take me in. I don't have to stay here and be the—what's the word?—canary."

He looked up, eyes haunted and hungry. "You're not a canary," he said.

"Then what am I?" Ren's voice was shaking now, the adrenaline leaking out and leaving only raw nerve.

Vincent didn't answer. He stared at the window again, watched the shadow that was and wasn't him.

Ren gave it one last try. "I need to know, Vincent. I need to know if I'm safe."

He looked at her, then at the floor, then back at his hands. The tremor was obvious now, the hunger a living thing gnawing through his composure. He opened his mouth to say something, closed it again, then forced the words out, one at a time.

"I don't know," he said. "I really, really don't."

For a long time, the only sound was the rain. It battered the glass, leaking into the seams of the night, as if determined to wear away every last bit of resistance. Ren gathered up her notebook, eyes still fixed on Vincent's face.

When she spoke, her voice was barely above a whisper. "If you ever—"

He shook his head, fast and hard. "I'd rather burn."

Ren nodded. "Good. Because I'll do it myself, if you can't."

She left then, not slamming the door, just closing it with the finality of a verdict. Vincent stayed by the window, watching the outline of himself fade into the dark.

On the coffee table, the book lay open to a page where someone—probably Mrs Barley, maybe even himself—had underlined a single, jagged sentence:

THE NEXT DRAFT ALWAYS EATS THE FIRST.

Vincent smiled, grim and hopeless.

Rain continued to paint the city in ribbons of rust and mercury. Inside Zara's flat, it sounded like a burial service—slow, deliberate, and impossible to ignore. The argument with Ren had burned through everything, left the air sharp as the first breath after a nosebleed. Vincent migrated from the armchair to the sofa, the springs accepting him with a creak that might have been a warning or just the last word in comfort.

He pressed his fingers to the fresh blisters, examined the moonscape of his own hand. The pain was less now, but the shape of it lingered—reminding him, every time he flexed, that there would always be something underneath.

He had never been good at silence, but tonight he let it spool out, until the only sounds were the rain and the slow, wet drip of a leak under the window. At last, he heard the shift of footsteps behind him—her return, maybe, or just his own memory lapping at the edges.

Ren stood in the threshold, arms crossed, eyes raw. She looked at him the way people look at weather reports, bracing for the worst and hoping for the statistical outlier.

"Are you just going to sit there and rot?" she asked.

Vincent shrugged, half-hearted. "It's a plan. Gets me out of paperwork, at least."

Ren moved closer, perched on the opposite end of the sofa, but angled herself to face him square-on. The candle on the coffee table, a lumpy pillar with more wick than wax, threw monster shadows on the wall and caught in the lines of Vincent's face, mapping out every year he'd tried to drink away.

He tried to joke, but his voice was flat. "I suppose now is the part where you tell me to man up."

Ren snorted. "You'd be useless at it. Just do what you always do—outlast everyone."

He ran a hand through his hair, wincing as he caught the edge of the burn. "You want the truth? I don't want this. I don't want to be... more vampire. It's bad enough being a Council cautionary tale. I'm not built for hunger."

She didn't reply right away, just studied his face like she was trying to work out if there was anything left worth saving.

"You could fight it," she said at last, voice low. "You could actually try for once, instead of cracking jokes and waiting for it to win."

Vincent almost laughed, but it caught in his throat. "I haven't won anything since the seventies, and that was a pub quiz."

She leaned in, lowering her voice. "You're not funny, Vincent. You're just scared."

He wanted to argue, but it wasn't worth it. He'd spent his life on the sharp end of clever words, and now they were just so much noise.

Ren reached for his hand, the one with the blisters. She didn't touch it—just hovered her palm above, as if the proximity alone might help. "If you go off the rails," she said, "I'll be there to stop you. But I'd rather you did it yourself. Take the fight back."

He looked at her, really looked, and for a moment he saw not just the Mark on her arm, or the familiar flicker of defiance, but the weariness of someone who had lived in the shadow of monsters her whole life and was only now learning to give the fear a name.

A noise at the door snapped the moment like a chalk line. Mrs Barley entered without a knock, her posture set to "military tribunal," her expression tuned for minimum empathy.

"Glad to see the suicide pact is coming along," she said, taking a seat in the armchair. "We have a situation."

She produced a Council folder from her bag and tossed it onto the table, scattering crisps and nuts. The file was thicker than usual, and the paper inside was already annotated in four different colours.

Vincent grunted, "Do we ever have anything else?"

Mrs Barley ignored him, fixing her gaze on Ren. "You'll want to pack some snacks. This is an overnight job."

Ren stood, her movements deliberate, already shifting into survival mode. She looked at Vincent, and this time there was no fear, only a tired solidarity.

"Come on, old man," she said. "Let's see if you can still keep up."

He dragged himself upright, rolling the sleeve down over the burn. He knew the hunger would follow, that the next draft of himself was waiting just around the corner. But for now, he had a purpose, and a witness.

FOURTEEN

Outside Ren's flat, Vincent leaned against the courtyard balustrade, eyes narrowed against the sodium glare and the prickling sense of future disaster. He checked his phone for the fourth time in as many minutes—no new messages, no notifications, no freelance executions scheduled. The only anomaly was the weather: a crisp, starlit sky, as if the smog had taken the night off.

Ren joined him, zipping her hoodie. The Mark on her arm was bandaged tight, but Vincent could see it pulse faint blue with every heartbeat. Mrs Barley was the last out. She locked the door, dropped the keys in her bag and immediately began to march towards the road.

"No straggling, you two."

If you asked, the night was waiting for something. Just as Vincent and Ren were about to fall into step behind Mrs Barley, the world ended, then rebooted, in a blast of sound and light.

A sports car—mid-aughts BMW, reupholstered in black

vinyl, undercarriage gleaming like a catwalk—slammed into the mouth of the courtyard. Headlights pulsed in time with the sub-bass, which rattled every window from here to Kilburn. The paint job was a wrap: neon decals that spelled out something between a QR code and a threat. The effect was less "midnight visitor" and more "IT technician's first rave."

Vincent was still cataloguing the stupidity of the car when the doors butterfly-opened and the Modernisers tumbled out.

There were three. The first was the leader by every metric: height, cheekbones, the kind of coat that looked like it had both a Patreon and a waiting list. His hair was platinum and sculpted, his skin so flawless it made Vincent's inner dermatologist weep. His eyes, when he found Vincent in the darkness, were rimmed in eyeliner so precise it could have been applied by laser.

The second Moderniser—shorter, sharper, gender-ambiguous in the way that cost money—carried a gimbal-stabilised phone rig. The third was almost too generic: brown hair, designer stubble, shoes that cost more than Vincent's monthly blood budget. But even he had a vibe—something in the way he carried himself, like every street was his personal runway.

The trio converged, leader in front, the others flanking like acolytes or security, though both looked too pretty to punch anything. The gimbal phone was already live, red LED winking, lens pointed at Vincent and co.

The leader spoke first, his voice a velvet-wrapped, influencer baritone: "Lupo the Lightless, in the flesh. Iconic." He extended a hand, manicured to the point of parody. "I'm Rafe. We're the welcoming committee."

Vincent stared at the hand, then at Rafe's face, then at the phone. "You're streaming this?"

Gimbal shrugged, flashing a gold-capped fang. "Content is currency, mate. And this is worth a few million hits."

Mrs Barley appeared at Vincent's side with the speed and precision of a retractable blade. "We were just on our way to see you. The meet-up was scheduled for 12:30, on neutral territory. Kindly explain why you're here, or I'll be forced to file a breach with your patron."

Rafe's lips twitched. "You must be Mrs Barley. We've read your files." He gestured at the air, as if summoning a hologram only he could see. "Sorry for the change of venue. We were just excited to get started."

Ren's hands shook a little, but her voice, when it came, was weirdly steady. "You're Modernisers. You work for Carmine's old network."

Rafe gave a little bow, somehow managing to make it look both ironic and sincere. "We prefer 'The Updated.' Moderniser is a Council term, and frankly, it's a bit retro."

Ren blinked, not missing a beat. "You're here to negotiate, then?"

"Negotiate, network, meme—whatever keeps the prophecy from eating the city," said Rafe, hands folded like a PR monk.

Vincent grimaced. "Then lose the phone."

Gimbal hesitated, thumb hovering over a control. "It's on mute. Well—audio's off. Video only."

Vincent bared his teeth, not bothering with the subtlety of a smile. "Switch it off or I switch you off."

Gimbal powered down. The camera, briefly alive with after-image, faded to black.

The brown-haired Moderniser stepped up, voice pitched low. "We brought gifts." He pulled a vacuum-sealed pouch from his coat, tossed it to Vincent. "O-negative, sourced last week, cold chain guaranteed. No strings, no taint."

Vincent caught it, weighed it, and without looking up, said, "You first."

Brown-hair grinned, showing smaller, more real fangs than Rafe. He tore open the second pouch, drank, and grimaced. "They always say it's 'single donor,' but it's never as fresh as the tap."

Vincent waited a beat, then drank his own. The taste was as promised: neutral, healthy, laced with just enough adrenaline to keep it interesting. He wiped his mouth with the back of his hand, then eyed the Modernisers with a mixture of annoyance and reluctant curiosity. "All right. You've delivered. Now what?"

Rafe smiled, teeth the white of TV static. "Now we connect with the old guard." He turned to Ren, eyes scanning her with the hungry precision of an algorithm. "You're the new Marked, aren't you?"

Ren's face went blank. She said nothing, just closed her notebook and hugged it to her chest.

Gimbal leaned in, phone still off. "She doesn't look like much."

Mrs Barley cleared her throat, loud enough to silence the street. "Protocol. All business is conducted inside. This is a residential area."

Rafe spread his arms. "After you."

Vincent hesitated. Then he noticed the flicker in the

shadows of the courtyard: Zara, half-materialised through the wall, blue and smirking.

He caught her eye. "You see this circus?"

Zara flickered fully in, dress phasing from Victorian mourning to PVC cocktail in three frames flat. "Oh, I see it," she said, voice echoing in the ears and nowhere else. "And I want a front row seat."

Vincent turned, nodded once to the others. "Let's go, then. You break anything, you clean it up."

The Modernisers followed, their footsteps echoing on the flagstones, neon reflections rippling across the windowpanes. For a moment, Vincent was back in 1987, when the only thing louder than the hunger was the synthpop, and he'd nearly lost an eye in a bar fight over a stolen pager.

Ren hung back, letting the vampires lead. She looked at Vincent, then at the blue-white afterimage of Zara, and then up at the sky, which still hadn't decided whether to join the party or just watch from a safe distance.

She followed, the Mark pulsing beneath her sleeve, already rewriting the script of the night.

The door to Ren's flat opened, and the future walked in, wrapped in leather, neon, and the certainty that nothing was ever really off the record.

Inside, the Modernisers spread across the flat like a designer virus. Every move was staged for maximum optics: Rafe took the battered mid-century sofa and sprawled, limbs artfully arranged, coat splayed like wings. Gimbal set up shop at the kitchen counter, mounting his ring light to a stack of cookbooks and adjusting the angle until it caught his cheekbones in "morning-after-glow." Brown-hair, who had introduced himself as Milo but responded equally to "bro," perched on the windowsill, one leg dangling, the other tucked under in a pose that would have required surgery for anyone less flexible.

Ren's flat was not built for this level of traffic, nor for the aesthetic onslaught. The only light came from the ring lamp and a cluster of half-burnt candles, which together made the room look like a séance thrown by the social media department of Vogue. Dust particles hung in the air, refracted through the ring, and settled in the immaculate hair of the guests without complaint.

Vincent stood by the window, hands deep in his coat pockets, scanning for exits that weren't currently blocked by undead influencers. He twitched every time the ring light strobed, which was often.

Mrs Barley occupied a patch of bare floor by the door, notebook out, glasses glinting. She alternated between glaring at the Modernisers and annotating their behaviour with the brisk efficiency of a police sketch artist documenting a particularly offensive mural.

Ren hung back, leaning against the kitchen wall, notebook open but pen silent. She watched the proceedings with the wary interest of a wildlife documentary producer, only occasionally breaking eye contact to check the Mark under her sleeve.

Zara was nowhere, and then suddenly everywhere. She flickered into the room above head height, spectral form stretched across the corner where the wall met the ceiling. The effect was unearthly, and faintly obscene, given the angle. She waved at Gimbal, who promptly tried to film her, but the phone glitched and spat static at the attempt.

"Nice kit," Zara said, eyeing the ring light. "But it's a little early in the night for cult recruitment, isn't it?"

Rafe grinned, baring teeth that were probably real but didn't look it. "There's no time like the present. Especially when the future is already trending."

Vincent growled—actual, literal growl, low and half-feral. "You didn't come here to sell us on your pyramid scheme. Cut to the chase."

Rafe did not rise to the bait. Instead, he produced a compact from an inside pocket, pretended to check his own reflection, then snapped it shut with a flourish. "Old-school. I love it. But you're right. Let's get down to business."

He stood, gliding to the centre of the room in a single, liquid movement. "Here's the pitch. You help us shape the narrative. Vampires can't hide forever, not with a prophecy eating the city and the Council playing catch-up. Better we own it. Make it art."

Gimbal, now holding the phone at chest level, added: "We're thinking rollout—short-form, snackable, networked to every major platform. Give them a story and you control the edit."

Vincent made a noise halfway between a laugh and a retch. "So, you want us to become a content house."

Milo, from the window: "Why not? You're already legend. Give the people what they want."

Mrs Barley interjected, voice dry as a salt flat. "Council

doctrine prohibits direct engagement with human media. You are, by definition, in breach."

Rafe rolled his eyes. "Council doctrine also prohibits recursion outbreaks and mass memory edits, but here we are. The world's changed. The old rules are dead."

Vincent turned to Ren, voice edged with contempt. "You buy this?"

Ren, who had been silent, closed her notebook with a snap. "They have reach. More than the Council, maybe more than Carmine. If you want to disrupt a network, you need to be louder than the signal."

Gimbal pointed at her, delighted. "She gets it. Influence isn't just a game, it's the board."

Vincent grimaced, then paced the perimeter of the room, circling behind the kitchen counter. He nearly tripped on a garlic clove left from the morning, and swore under his breath.

Milo leaned in. "Look, we know you're not in love with the brand. But Council's got you boxed, Carmine's rewriting the script, and the only way to win is to make them play your game."

Mrs Barley, writing as she spoke: "You are reckless. Undisciplined. But not malicious. Potentially useful, despite appearances."

Rafe put a hand to his heart, mock-offended. "We're just here to survive. Same as you."

Zara, still floating overhead, chimed in. "Council hates them. Which means they're probably useful."

Vincent looked up at her, then back at Rafe. "You think you can meme your way out of the prophecy?"

Rafe smirked. "I think we can crowdsource a solution, if we go viral enough."

Vincent's expression soured, but Ren stepped forward, arms folded. "Suppose we do help you. What's in it for us?"

Gimbal produced a phone, flicked through a half-dozen screens, and turned it so the group could see. "We distract, you act. We eat the narrative, you get room to breathe. Council won't see you coming if they're watching us."

Milo added: "And you get to write your own ending. Isn't that what every vampire wants?"

Vincent looked at the phone, then at Ren, then at Mrs Barley. "I'm not joining your TikTok coven."

Rafe grinned. "You already did. Just by letting us in."

There was a silence, brief but total, broken only by the faint hiss of the ring light and the whine of the dishwasher.

Mrs Barley snapped her notebook shut. "We will consider your proposal. For now, you are guests, nothing more."

Rafe nodded, all business. "No pressure. But the clock's ticking, and Carmine's not slowing down."

Zara descended, solidifying just long enough to blow Gimbal a ghostly kiss. "Play nice, boys. I'd hate to see you go out in a blaze of memes."

The Modernisers exchanged a look, all three at once, the way animals did when they sensed blood in the water. Rafe extended a hand again, this time to Ren. "If you want in, just say the word."

Ren hesitated, then took it, grip firm. "We'll let you know."

Rafe held her gaze, eyes just this side of sincere. "Looking forward to it."

The Modernisers let themselves out, neon coats shimmering

in the hallway light. As the door closed behind them, the apartment seemed to exhale, the tension leaking away like a punctured air mattress.

Vincent slumped into the armchair, head in his hands. "The end times used to be more dignified."

Zara perched on the back of the chair, spectral fingers running through Vincent's hair. "Maybe, but they were a lot less fun."

Ren went to the window, watching as the BMW peeled out, music already cranked back up to eleven.

Mrs Barley stood, squared her shoulders, and spoke to the room: "We are not collaborating with anarchists. But we will use them. Every asset is an opportunity."

Vincent looked at her, then at Ren. "Asset or not, they're dangerous. But so is Carmine. So's the Council."

Ren nodded, fingers tracing the Mark under her sleeve. "Then we play all sides. And we do it better than they expect."

For a long time, no one spoke. The city outside thrummed, a low static of potential disaster.

Zara broke the silence, voice pitched halfway between mischief and prophecy. "Let's make history, then."

The flat was quiet, but the bassline from the Modernisers' car still vibrated the windows. It would be hours before anyone slept, and days before they'd admit how much the pitch had changed everything.

But in that moment, in the blue-lit aftermath, Vincent almost believed they might pull it off.

Almost.

FIFTEEN

At the Council's archives, Vincent followed Mrs Barley down the central aisle, her step brisk and eerily silent on the cracked vinyl tiles. The light from above caught her hair, rendering it halo-bright one second and ghost-grey the next. Vincent found himself keeping time with the rhythm of her shoulders, as if matching her pace might ward off the chill that had settled between his vertebrae the moment they'd crossed the threshold.

"Do you come here often?" he muttered, voice pitched for maximum irreverence. "Or is this just a first-date kind of venue?"

Mrs Barley didn't break stride. "If you'd filed your own requisitions, you'd know I spend most evenings down here. Some of us do actual work."

They emerged into the main hall, a space that might once have hosted balls or executions, but was now repurposed as the central intake for the entire undercity's worth of records. The ceiling rose out of sight, beams vanished into shadow, and somewhere in the haze above, the fluorescent fixtures flickered in time with the slow, agonised death of the planet's power grid.

The lone night clerk, species indeterminate, slouched behind a glass-fronted counter littered with highlighter corpses and instant noodle wrappers. He looked up only when Mrs Barley rapped the countertop with a closed fist.

"Research access," she said, presenting her Council credentials with the same gravity as a badge at a crime scene.

The clerk examined the ID, then Vincent, then the ID again. "Is he with you?"

Mrs Barley nodded. "He's a temp. On loan from Legal."

Vincent winked at the clerk, who responded by yawning so wide his jaw clicked. "No eating in the stacks. If you're caught, you'll have to log the violation yourself."

"Wouldn't dream of it," Vincent said, but the clerk had already returned to scrolling on his phone with a speed that suggested either chronic boredom or a supernatural thumb.

Mrs Barley signed the ledger with her own pen—she did not, Vincent noted, even consider using the one on the counter —and handed Vincent a visitor's lanyard. It was sticky, and bore the faded outline of a cartoon bat.

"Really pulls the look together," he said, clipping it to his lapel.

Mrs Barley ignored this and navigated the maze of stacks with the certainty of a Victorian ghost retracing the route to her own murder. Vincent trailed behind, counting the ways the archives had not changed in seven centuries: the smell of old glue and older politics, the sense that nothing down here had ever really died, just reclassified.

They passed through the first two aisles in silence. The

further they went, the less reliable the lighting became, until even Vincent's vision struggled to parse the fine print. He caught glimpses of labels: POSTWAR CLEAN-UP; METROPOLITAN FEEDING RIGHTS; PROPHECY HOLDING (CLASSIFIED). Most files were locked behind mesh grilles or triple-pinned with red thread, but a few shelves slouched open, overstuffed with binders that had surrendered to entropy.

Mrs Barley stopped at a junction and fished a sheet of paper from her sleeve. It was a requisition form, pre-filled and annotated in her own spidery hand. She consulted it, then made a hard left, pausing only to tug a rolling ladder out from between two heaving cabinets. She ascended without looking back.

Vincent leaned against the shelves, eyeing the cramped reading desk below. "I'd offer to spot you, but I suspect you'd take offense."

"Correct," Mrs Barley said, already four rungs up and scanning the upper tiers. She selected a binder with a rusted lock, then another, then a third, dropping each onto the desk with the finality of a death sentence. When she descended, she was breathing harder, but her face had not moved from its default setting: neutral-to-murderous.

She motioned for Vincent to sit, then set about opening the files in a precise, almost surgical sequence. "Help yourself," she said. "You can start with the relevant incidents. I'll handle the cross-referencing."

Vincent eyed the first binder: MODERNISER EVENTS, 2014–PRESENT. The cover bore a Council stamp so faded it could have been an antique, but the contents inside were pristine, every page laminated, every entry indexed. He flipped through the first dozen reports: a Soho warehouse party gone spectral, a Shoreditch protest that had ended in "viral exsanguination," a Moderniser-run "pop-up" in Camden that had collapsed into full-on prophecy riot.

Each report followed the same pattern. Incident, time, location. Witnesses, evidence, a summary of containment. Always, at the end, a line in bold: CONCLUSION: GLAMOUR MALFUNCTION / MASS HYSTERIA. And the verdict: *Council recommends no further action.*

Vincent frowned, then flipped another page. The reports grew more detailed, more manic, until entire paragraphs were blacked out with the kind of marker you could smell from the next table. "They're not even trying to be subtle," he said, running a finger along the redacted lines.

Mrs Barley glanced over. "They don't have to. No one outside the Council ever reads these."

Vincent switched to the next file: HIGHGATE ANOMALY, 1998–2021. He recognised some of the names: case officers who had vanished, locations he'd once staked out under cover of moonlight and idiocy. The pattern was the same. Occult incident. Escalation. Resolution—always by "dispersal," "containment," or, in two cases, "strategic burn."

Vincent exhaled, a slow whistle. "So they've known about the recursion for years."

"Decades," Mrs Barley corrected. She had her phone out now, surreptitiously photographing each page with a discrete click and a flick of her thumb. "They've been misfiling it as viral meme activity or, if it was pre-social media, a PR disaster."

Vincent reached for the last file: PARLIAMENTARY DISRUPTIONS, 2007–CURRENT. He expected to see the usual—rowdy Moderniser protests, a few well-publicised incidents, perhaps a line about "digital destabilisation." What he got instead was a series of entries marked URGENT. The earliest was from 2012, the most recent from this week. Each described a near-identical sequence: a speech, a glitch, then a sudden, contagious outbreak of prophecy among the crowd. Symptoms included "subliminal transmission," "compulsive repetition of phrases," and "acute memory overwrite." Containment was always "successful," but the follow-up pages told a different story.

Vincent leaned in. The paper was thin, brittle, and reeked of old ozone. He ran his finger down the timeline until it stopped on an entry from five years prior.

SUBJECT: MEMBER OF PARLIAMENT—EDITED OUT OF EXISTENCE.

INCIDENT: Spontaneous recitation of Carmine's Prophecy during live broadcast. Witnesses: hundreds. Digital copies: deleted within 48 hours. Subject remembered by Council only.

Vincent looked up at Mrs Barley. "They're not just hiding it. They're letting it propagate, then rewriting the records after the fact."

She nodded, lips pressed to a line so thin it seemed to have given up on even the pretence of humanity. "Standard operating procedure. The more witnesses, the faster the clean-up. Public memory is just another asset."

Vincent's grip whitened on the edge of the page. "But the recursion's getting worse. If Carmine's back, he's feeding on this—on their own denials."

"Precisely," Mrs Barley said, voice low. She reached across

him, snapping a few more photos, then flipped the page to reveal the original report beneath. The handwriting was different, older. The date was 1973.

"The Council's known about Carmine since the seventies," she said. "Possibly earlier. But the more the recursion mutates, the more elaborate the cover-up. Look at the edits—see how the terminology changes?"

Vincent examined the two pages. In the earlier report, the incident was listed as "Spectral Speech Event," with a notation about "potential viral properties." The new one simply called it a "Parliamentary Glamour Malfunction." The entire section about prophecy was gone, replaced by a paragraph on "possible adverse drug reaction."

He closed the file and leaned back, letting the chair creak under his weight. "So, we've been chasing our own tails. Or Carmine's, depending on the draft."

Mrs Barley didn't answer, but there was a grim satisfaction in her eyes. She snapped the last binder shut, stacked them with the care of a bomb disposal technician, and slid her phone back into her jacket.

"I'm guessing the next phase is a memory wipe," Vincent said. "Standard procedure, right?"

Mrs Barley gathered the files. "Not tonight. They're expecting us to be thorough, but not imaginative."

Vincent grinned, teeth bright in the half-light. "They're in for a disappointment."

She tucked the files under her arm, then gestured at the way out. "After you. We'll need to duplicate the evidence before the next shift. Then destroy the rest."

Vincent stood, stretching, and for the first time since

entering the archives, he felt something close to hope. Not much, but enough to get him through the next few hours.

As they retraced their steps, Mrs Barley paused at the counter to return the binders. The clerk looked up, registering her presence with the interest of someone watching paint dry via time-lapse.

"Find what you needed?" he asked, tone bored but not unfriendly.

Mrs Barley offered a thin smile. "Everything and more."

Vincent fished the lanyard off his collar, setting it down with a theatrical sigh. "You ought to get better lighting back there," he said, jerking his chin toward the stacks.

The clerk smirked. "We like it dim. Hides the dust."

Vincent looked at Mrs Barley, who was already out the door, then back at the clerk. "Cheers," he said, and followed her into the corridor.

Outside, the chill hit harder, but Vincent barely noticed. He watched as Mrs Barley, with a quick flick of her wrist, uploaded the photos to a secure drive, then dropped the phone into her pocket with the kind of finality that made it clear the device was now a time bomb.

"You trust the Council's IT not to trace that?" he asked.

Mrs Barley's expression did not change. "No. But they're not the only ones with access."

Vincent laughed, genuine this time. "Remind me never to piss you off."

Mrs Barley regarded him for a moment, then said, "You'd have to try much harder."

They made their way to the lift, which took so long to arrive that Vincent could almost hear the centuries turning over in its gears. As they waited, Mrs Barley fixed him with a stare that could have frozen a lesser man to the marrow.

"Next step?" she said.

Vincent thought for a moment. "Zara's. I Mean Ren's. Anywhere but here."

Mrs Barley nodded, as if she'd already anticipated the answer. The lift arrived, doors squealing open, and they stepped inside.

As the doors closed, Vincent glanced at the files in her arms, then caught the shadow of his own face in the tarnished steel.

"They think we're expendable," he said, softly.

Mrs Barley regarded his reflection, but decided to ignore it. "Let's prove them wrong."

The lift juddered, shuddered, then began its slow climb back to the surface.

Above, the city waited, restless as ever, while the evidence of its secret history pulsed in the dark, ready for the next edit.

Mrs Barley commandeered the kitchen table with the ease of a long-term occupier: council files and battered legal pads in a fan across one end, Vincent's ancient laptop and a wine-stained coaster at the other, and a small, unamused Ren squeezed between, her knees nearly brushing the bin pedal. The overhead lamp buzzed and flickered, flicking sickly light across the stacks, while the rest of the flat maintained its habitual gloom.

Mrs Barley's ritual began with the lining up of four battered mugs, each with the Council's crest eroded to different stages of meaninglessness. She poured the wine, not for the ceremony of it, but to keep Vincent's hands occupied and Ren's from shaking. The kitchen window rattled in its casing—whether from the wind or from Zara's imminent arrival, it was hard to say.

Vincent, chair tipped back against the fridge, thumbed through the first set of photos Mrs Barley had sent to his phone. "You know, the digital age has done wonders for Council record-keeping. They can now lose evidence in two places at once."

"Three, if you count the printer graveyard in the sub-basement," Mrs Barley said, not looking up from her own pile of notes.

Ren closed her hands over her mug, the Mark on her forearm throbbing a faint blue under the sleeve. She'd slept perhaps an hour in the last forty, and her voice had acquired a sandpaper edge. "What did you find?"

Mrs Barley laid out the evidence like a dealer in a high-stakes poker game. "Pattern's clear. Every major Moderniser incident, from Shoreditch through Parliament, was forecast and documented years before anyone responded. Council protocol? File it as 'hysteria' and hope the mortals forget by Monday."

She pointed to a cluster of dates, each highlighted in a sickly yellow. "See this? That's the same phrase, recycled through seven different committees. 'Glamour malfunction'. 'Urban panic'. 'Unusual meteorological event'. All after-action, all signed by the same two proxies. It's a botched cover-up, but at scale."

Ren's lips pressed white, but she managed, "So they've been —what, just letting it spread?"

Vincent swirled the wine, watching the sediment spiral.

"Bureaucracy's one true innovation: outsource the problem to time and hope sheer laziness finishes the job."

Ren scowled at him. "It's not funny, Vincent. People died. Are dying."

He met her gaze, the lines around his mouth etched a little deeper. "That's bureaucracy, kid. Better paperwork than truth."

The overhead bulb surged, then flickered out entirely, leaving the room lit only by Zara's arrival—a corona of cold blue, her outline phased three-quarters into the world and perched, for reasons best left unexamined, above the refrigerator.

She grinned down at them, arms folded, her gaze snagging on Mrs Barley's documents. "You found the good stuff," she said. "I remember that one—" she jabbed a finger at the Shoreditch file, "—absolute carnage. Took three months to get the blood out of the fibreboard."

Mrs Barley did not dignify this with a response, instead pushing the file toward Vincent. "What matters is the chain of custody. Every edit, every redaction, is deliberate. The Council's not just hiding Carmine. They're helping him."

Ren's face twisted, knuckles whitening as she gripped the edge of the table. "They're letting people die, just so mortals won't ask questions?"

Zara floated down, settling next to Ren in a waft of freezer chill. "That's what the Council does best. They don't care about people. They care about protocol. And," she flicked her eyes to Vincent, "they care about villains. Makes the story neater."

Vincent snorted, but it was hollow. "Congratulations, Lupo. You're the villain of their story."

Ren looked up, tears starting at the corner of her eyes, but burning off before they had a chance to fall. "This is sick. We should just—just burn it all down."

Mrs Barley snapped her notebook shut with a force that echoed off the bare walls. "Not yet. We go public, we lose control. They erase us, or worse—frame us for the next incident. No, we need to get ahead of the recursion. Cut Carmine's leverage before it hits the next news cycle."

Vincent drained his mug, then set it down with care. "And how exactly do you propose we do that? The Council's got eyes everywhere, and Carmine is at least two moves ahead."

Mrs Barley looked at the team—Vincent, Ren, Zara—and for the first time since the night began, her mask cracked into something almost like hope. "We rewrite the story," she said. "We flip the script. No more running. No more hiding. If the Council wants a narrative, we'll give them one. But it's going to be ours."

A silence fell, but it was a charged one, every particle of it bristling with intent.

Zara smirked, her glow shifting from blue to ultraviolet at the edges. "Now you're talking my language."

Ren straightened, wiping her eyes with the sleeve. The Mark was bright now, pulsing in time with her breath. "Let's do it."

Vincent considered the files, the wine, and his own battered knuckles, which really should have healed by now. Then he shrugged, slow and inevitable. "What's the worst that could happen?"

Mrs Barley stood, gathering the files into a single, lethal dossier. "Then we're agreed. We control the draft."

It wasn't a shout, but it was loud enough to make the windows vibrate.

They sat for a long time, the four of them, plotting the next steps with the grim delight of people who had nothing left to lose and everything to gain by lying, cheating, and surviving a little longer than the rest.

And then the lights went out.

SIXTEEN

The light's extinction left a hush so absolute that even the spectral footnotes retreated into nothing, unwilling to risk becoming part of the next story. For a moment, it was not clear whether the chill in the room was ghost, prophecy, or just the prelude to a blackout.

Then Ren hissed and doubled over, clutching her forearm. The Editor's Mark, previously a shade of illicit office blue, now burned with a voltage closer to surgical laser. It bled through the fabric of her sleeve, casting enough light to etch afterimages onto the backs of her own eyelids. The pain was more than pain: it was editorial, a red-pen correction that ran up her nerves and into the base of her skull.

Vincent, eyes still adjusting, felt his own teeth begin to lengthen, a subcutaneous itch announcing itself with slow, inevitability. He suppressed the urge to bare them—not the time, not the company—though the hunger that usually snarked in the background now roared with the certainty of a deadline. He pressed himself away from the wall, glass trembling in hand, and exhaled through his nose like a boxer approaching the final round.

Zara had not so much moved as reconfigured her place in the room. One instant she was at the table's head, the next she hovered directly above Ren, her own glow in strange sync with the Mark's. She did not cast a shadow; even the blue of her outline seemed to deny the possibility of negative space. Reaching down, she let her translucent palm pass through Ren's arm, and for a second the pain abated—then doubled, as if the ghost's touch had given the Mark permission to express its full repertoire.

"He's tethered to you, too," Zara murmured, voice gentle but with a high, mosquito whine of excitement. "You're the early-access edition. Hot off the press."

Ren glared, jaw locked against the urge to scream. "Tell that to my nervous system."

Zara smiled, but it was not the smile of a mentor; it was the unsettling pride of an artist watching their medium finally react. "This is what he did," she said, staring straight through Ren and at something that lived in the marrow. "Carmine seeded every edition. Marked every reader. It's not just prophecy—he's turning us into a chain of rewrites. Whoever holds the Mark is the next node in the network."

Vincent didn't like where this was going, but the alternatives were worse.

Zara's gaze sharpened, and for the first time, the sarcasm failed to bounce. "Anyone who's ever quoted the prophecy is part of the script. The more it's recited, the more the story converges on itself." Her form solidified for a fraction of a heartbeat, blue neon flickering to a vivid, unbearable white. "He's hungry, Vincent. And he's already editing you."

Mrs Barley, who had spent the interim shuffling her pens and Post-it notes into defensive formations, snapped her notebook shut with a noise that could have woken the flat's several dead plants. She adjusted her glasses, then regarded the group with a stare that refused to admit panic. "Then we prepare as if he's already in the room," she said, voice flat and unsentimental. "This is not an outbreak. This is a possession."

Ren slumped back, arm still throbbing, the blue now suffused with a veinwork of fresh red. "I don't want to be in his story," she said, softer than before. "I'd rather write my own ending."

Mrs Barley nodded once. "Then we take control of the script. First step: contain the Mark, limit exposure. Second: disrupt the narrative. We cannot let the next phase propagate."

Vincent finished his wine in a single, unlovely gulp. "And if he's already in our heads?"

Mrs Barley looked him dead in the eye. "Then we out-write him."

A silence dropped, thick as paste, over the room. Even Zara seemed at a loss, the hard edges of her form dissolving into mist as she hovered, undecided, above the table. The heap of annotated manuscripts began to twitch in time with the pulse of Ren's arm, every shuffle and creak a possible incursion from the other side.

Vincent watched the Mark, then the lamp, then the lamp's

reflection in the blank TV screen. "He's watching us," he said, and the words felt uncomfortably correct. "Every time we speak, every time we remember. He's always one line ahead."

Zara's lips curled, as if daring the ghost of Carmine to do better. "That's the thing about being dead," she said, voice thin and sharp. "It only makes you harder to edit."

Mrs Barley rose, smoothing her skirt with a single, deliberate movement. "We go dark for tonight," she said. "No more discussion, no more written record. Tomorrow, we take the fight to him."

Ren hugged her arm, Mark hidden but still leaking enough light to silhouette her veins. "He'll follow," she said. "He always does."

Mrs Barley's eyes were almost kind. "Let him. But we choose the battlefield."

Vincent let his fangs lengthen, just for the satisfaction of it, and bit the edge of his glass hard enough to score the surface. "If he wants a scene, we'll give him a performance."

Zara drifted toward the window, blue light pooling around her feet. "He'll like that," she said. "He always did have a taste for drama."

Mrs Barley herded Ren to the inner room, gentle but unyielding. Vincent remained behind, surveying the flat—its piles of paper, its phantom afterglow, the faint taste of prophecy still hanging in the air. He wondered what it meant to be edited by a ghost, and whether, in the end, any version of himself would make it to the final cut.

The darkness persisted, pressing in at the edges. For once, Vincent found comfort in it.

Tomorrow, Carmine would escalate. But for tonight, the only thing to do was survive, and hope that when the next scene began, he would still recognise his own lines.

And somewhere, in the pile of living paper, a new paragraph began to write itself—patient, inevitable, and ready for the next edit.

SEVENTEEN

The Moderniser *bar du jour* was not, technically speaking, a bar at all. The venue, a fourth-storey rooftop atop an old Ministry of Justice annexe, had been repurposed by someone with a working knowledge of guerilla hospitality and a sick sense of humour. The main attraction was the view: Parliament, the river, and the smog-snagged skyline—all of it best appreciated through a haze of bass and backlit vodka. Someone had even installed LED crosses along the railings, alternating between ultraviolet and blood-orange, so that the crowd could enjoy the illusion of a permanent afterparty at the scene of their own resurrection.

Vincent hated it on principle.

He hunched at the edge of the crowd, half in the open, half concealed by a potted olive tree, the base of which, had become an ashtray. He'd worn his least arresting coat, a charcoal thing with just enough polyester to resist bloodstains, and he nursed a glass of club soda in order to pass as "high-functioning alco-holic" rather than "ancient, walking cautionary tale."

Ren was beside him, perched on a barstool with her knees up, hoodie drawn tight around her face. She sipped bottled water and clicked away on her battered phone, running back-ground searches on the evening's guest list. The Mark on her arm had faded to a dull aquamarine, but every time a Moderniser passed within three metres, it flared up like a mood ring with an attachment disorder.

Mrs Barley, who had never looked more out of place, patrolled the outer perimeter with an umbrella (it was not rain-ing) and a clipboard (it was, in fact, a clipboard). She moved with the economy of a shopping centre security officer at closing time, her gaze raking over the crowd and the horizon at five-second intervals. If anyone tried to make contact, she deployed the kind of withering smile that could sink a medium-sized company.

Zara was, as usual, a problem for other people to solve. She flickered in and out of view near the roof's edge, half-substance and half gossip, watching the crowd with the carnivorous delight of someone who had once set fire to a wedding for the drama of it. Occasionally, she would drift close enough for Ren to catch a chill, but mostly she just watched and waited for the inevitable disaster.

The crowd was a study in cultivated apathy, all of them there to see and be seen, most of them more interested in the spectacle of their own performance than the actual event. The Modernisers were thick on the ground tonight: pale, over-acces-sorised, and in various stages of feeding or being fed upon. A few had brought mortal guests—arm candy, blood dolls, or the sort of goth tourists who would selfie themselves into a shallow grave by dawn.

Vincent hated them most of all.

He glanced sidelong at Ren. "Remind me why we're at the world's worst cocktail lounge queue, again?"

She didn't look up from the screen. "Because this is where the recursion started last time. Council says it's due to pop off at midnight, plus or minus thirty minutes, depending on the influencer count."

Vincent's eyes rolled so hard they nearly unmoored from their sockets. "I'd take the heat death of the universe over another minute of this music."

"It's not music," Ren said. "It's marketing. You can tell by the way the bass only drops when someone tags the location."

Vincent would have said something meaner, but at that exact moment, the bar's PA system cut out mid-beat. The sound of five dozen conversations spiked upward, then stuttered, then fell away as the house lights dimmed.

On the far side of the rooftop, near the fire escape, a ring of Modernisers had clustered around an old stone table—likely filched from the Ministry's original boardroom and now serving as an altar to viral attention spans. On the table were drinks, phones, and a single, antique ledger bound in what looked like human skin and the regrets of lesser mortals.

Vincent narrowed his gaze. "Is that—?"

Ren nodded. "Council-issued. Edition two, printed before they started watermarking the margins."

He winced. "Brave of them to bring it to a fight."

She shrugged. "Maybe they're bait."

The air shifted—Vincent felt it before he saw it. The weight of a new pressure front, the subtle uptick in humidity and despair. He checked the time: 23:53. Of course.

Mrs Barley materialised at his elbow, all business. "They're late," she said, as if commenting on a train rather than a potential apocalypse.

"They're Modernisers," Ren said. "They only show up on time if there's a camera."

"Or a prophecy," said Mrs Barley, with a glance at the table. "That's the vector."

Vincent reached into his coat, pulled out a dog-eared Moleskine, and flipped it open to the last clean page. He didn't know why he bothered; the last time he'd tried to document a live prophecy, the notebook had caught fire. But habit was a comfort, even when it tried to kill you.

The crowd began to cluster, subtly at first, then with the desperate energy of people who knew they were about to be upstaged. The Modernisers at the altar raised their phones in unison, their ring lights casting a sickly pallor over the surrounding faces. Someone in the crowd started a slow chant, which was equal parts ominous and pathetic.

Zara's spectral form slid up next to Ren. "You're about to get your spectacle," she murmured, her voice vibrating through three dimensions at once. "See the big one, platinum hair, ringmaster coat? That's the host. Name's Cassian, but he's gone by at least four different handles in the last six months. Council thinks he's the next draft of Carmine's favoured puppet."

Ren squinted, checked her phone, and nodded. "He's in the files. Background in marketing, two stints in rehab. Allegedly."

"Allegedly," Vincent repeated, "is the only true constant."

They watched as Cassian lifted the ledger and, with a

theatrical flourish, opened it to the midpoint. The crowd hushed. A single, blue-white beam from a phone spotlight illuminated the page. Cassian began to read, but the words were not in any language Vincent recognised, at least not at first.

It started in the teeth. Vincent felt his jaw tighten, fangs lengthen—not the controlled, practical extension he could manage at will, but a raw, involuntary surge. His gums split, blood pooling under the tongue. The same was happening all around: a ripple effect, fang after fang breaching the surface, like sharks in a blood-warmed bay.

The prophecy slithered out of the air, crawling across the steel railings, the glassware, even the LED crosses. Words etched themselves onto the surfaces in fine, black script, as if the bar had become a palimpsest and the prophecy was the only thing that mattered.

Ren jerked back, her Mark now bright enough to light the inside of her hoodie. "He's jumping," she said. "It's using the hardware. Every phone, every speaker, every live feed—he's everywhere."

Mrs Barley produced a fountain pen from nowhere and started writing, her hand moving faster than should be possible. "He's not after the vampires," she muttered. "He's after the narrative. The mortals are the battery."

Vincent looked up in time to see Cassian's face glitch, just for a second, as if someone had dropped a frame in the middle of reality. His features blurred, flickered, then reconstituted with a smile that showed every tooth, all the way back to the wisdoms.

He spoke, and the voice was not his. It was Carmine's,

stretched and layered, amplified through the combined larynx of everyone present.

"History is not a wound to be healed. It is a feast for the future. Bleed the past, and let the marrow nourish what comes next."

A shock ran through the crowd. Mortals dropped first: eyes rolled back, arms rigid, every one of them chanting the last line with perfect, unbroken synchrony. Vampires followed, many collapsing as if poleaxed, the unlucky few still standing now running full-on prophecy virus, words pouring out of their mouths like they'd been dipped in printer ink.

Zara clapped, delighted. "It's a good one! He's getting better at the climax."

Ren doubled over, her Mark pulsing with wild, arrhythmic flashes. "He's rewriting them. All of them. It's not a prophecy, it's a fucking firmware update."

Vincent spat blood, his own voice layered and hoarse. "How do we stop it?"

Mrs Barley did not answer. Instead, she threw her notebook into the air, pages fanning out and catching the etched prophecy as they fell. The paper caught fire, burning blue, and the ash floated upward, spelling the original line in negative as it was consumed.

The LED crosses began to short out, strobing between ultraviolet and stroboscopic orange, the effect so intense that even the vampires started to cower. On the far side of the altar, a handful of Modernisers regained control, shaking off the effect and running for the stairs. One tripped, landed face-first in a planter, and did not get back up.

Cassian—no, Carmine—raised his arms and let the ledger slam shut. The air shuddered.

Mrs Barley leaned toward Vincent, voice so low it barely reached over the sound of the crowd. "Disrupt the hardware. Break the circuit, and you break the loop."

Vincent didn't waste a second. He grabbed the nearest phone, stomped it into the decking, and kicked a second into the next postcode. Ren, on her feet again, yanked the sound system's main cable and watched as the speakers popped and hissed, then died.

It worked, a little. The mortals blinked, some collapsing in heaps, others swaying as if waking from a very bad dream. But Carmine was still there, inhabiting Cassian's body with all the entitlement of an unpaid intern.

Vincent squared his shoulders, bared his teeth, and said, "If you want to rewrite history, you'll have to start with me."

Carmine/Cassian grinned. "You're already the edit, Vincent. Everything that happens now is just a footnote."

The Modernisers—those left standing—began to move in unison, shoulders squared, eyes wide and milky, mouths moving in perfect sync as if they'd all decided to update their firmware at the same moment.

The mortals followed, the infection slower but no less final. Those who'd been closest to Cassian's altar now jerked and shambled, lips splitting into uncanny, rictus grins. The glamour had collapsed; what was left was a menagerie of hungers, each desperate to be first in the queue.

Vincent barely had time to process the new hierarchy of threat before a rail-thin Moderniser lunged at him, teeth bared, hands curled into claws. He sidestepped, grabbing the kid by the collar and flinging him into a table, the wood splintering with a sound that would have made any carpenter weep. Two more came at him from either side, one clutching a broken bottle, the other wielding a set of acrylic nails like scalpels.

He took the hit from the bottle—glass slashed across his jaw, cold and shallow—then turned, planted an elbow in the acrylic assassin's ribs, and shoved her into the nearest group of moaning, half-upright mortals.

"Mrs Barley!" he yelled, glancing toward the last place he'd seen her.

She was busy. The umbrella, now used as a truncheon, arced through the air and caught an attacking Moderniser right in the temple. The body dropped, twitching, and the umbrella spun in her grip like an executioner's axe. With her free hand, she had produced a red Swingline stapler—classic office issue, the kind that could outlast most nuclear events—and used it to staple the lapel of a revenant's coat to his own chest. He struggled, but Mrs Barley simply hammered the staple flat with the heel of her hand and moved on, dispatching threats with the efficiency of a woman who had never once left a meeting unfinished.

Vincent would have watched for longer, but the next wave hit.

Ren was not so lucky. One of the mortals—female, hair in a slicked bun, eyes as flat and empty as a phone on 1%—grabbed her by the neck and lifted her bodily off the ground, slamming her into the railing so hard the metal sang. Ren gasped, feet scrabbling at the decking, hands clawing at the wrist. The Mark on her arm flared, a vertical spike of white so hot it cast afterimages on the inside of Vincent's skull.

"Let go!" Ren screamed, but the voice that came out wasn't hers—it was layered, chorus-like, Carmine's stanzas curling off her tongue and into the air:

"The flesh is memory. The blood is record. Let it write you, line by line."

The mortal's grip tightened. Ren's face went deep blue, then a shade that wasn't on any human spectrum. Vincent bolted, ignoring the revenant who managed to catch him just below the ribcage with a broken table leg. He yanked the woman off Ren, twisting the arm until something snapped, and hurled her over the railing. She didn't even scream—just hit the ground three floors down with a noise like wet newsprint.

Ren collapsed to the boards, gasping. The Mark was still blazing, pulsing in time with her heart, every beat slower than the last.

Vincent bent down, risked a look at her face. She was pale, eyes nearly rolled back, lips moving as if reciting from a script only she could see.

"Hold on," he hissed, and pressed his hand over her Mark, trying to shield it from whatever was burning her alive. The pain was instant and total—heat travelled up his own arm, setting every nerve ending on fire, but he didn't stop.

From behind, Carmine's voice echoed again—not through speakers, not through mortals, but through the mouth of Cassian, who had somehow struggled upright. The ledger, burned and black, clung to his hands, fingers fused to the cover by blood and melted ink.

"You think you can break the cycle?" Carmine spat. "You were the cycle. The Bloodbard. The edit. Every story needs a sacrifice."

Vincent looked at Ren, then at Mrs Barley, who was now holding off three Modernisers at once, umbrella a blur. He knew what was coming, but he did it anyway.

He let the fangs come, full length, and bit his own wrist, tearing open a vein with practiced efficiency. He pressed the wound to Ren's mouth and forced her lips open, ignoring her attempts to resist. Blood spilled in, hot and spiked with adrenaline, and for a moment Vincent thought she'd choke. But then her throat convulsed, and she swallowed.

The effect was immediate. The Mark absorbed the blood, first hissing, then glowing a deep, infernal red. Ren's eyes snapped open, pupils blown wide, and she let out a gasp that ended in a scream.

Carmine's voice, riding the air, faltered.

"You see?" Vincent barked, voice raw. "We can change the ending. Even if we have to cheat."

He pulled Ren up, blood still dripping from his wrist. She coughed, spat, then wiped her mouth with the back of her hand, staring at Vincent with something between horror and gratitude.

"Don't ever do that again," she croaked.

Vincent grinned, though the muscles in his face screamed protest. "One-time offer. Next time, you're on your own."

The air shimmered. Cassian's body—no, Carmine's echo—advanced, dragging the ledger like a wounded limb. The words on the cover crawled, reconfiguring, then split open down the spine. A blade, thin and black as a negative, emerged from the gap, the edge jagged with letters.

Vincent squared up. "Come on then. You want an edit war, let's have it."

Carmine obliged, swinging the word-blade in a horizontal arc. Vincent ducked, but the tip caught his shoulder, opening a wound that gushed both blood and something darker—liquid script, pooling on the boards and eating through the deck like acid.

Vincent roared, swung a fist at Carmine's face. The impact was solid, but Carmine didn't bleed; instead, his features flickered, every hit replacing one line with another, as if the punch had forced a glitch in the underlying draft.

Behind them, the crowd had devolved into pure violence. Mrs Barley had switched to the stapler full time, eyes wild but focused, moving through the revenants like a bureaucratic tornado. Zara phased in and out, sometimes tripping an attacker, sometimes flickering through a wall to shout directions at Ren.

"Now, Ren!" she called, voice split into three harmonics. "Disrupt the Mark!"

Ren, on her knees, pressed both hands to her arm. The Mark, wild and red, pulsed harder. She clenched her jaw, then began to recite—not Carmine's lines, but her own. Fragments from every report, every failed Council memo, every bit of bureaucracy that had been forced into her skull since this nightmare began.

"Observation," she said. "Subject exhibits recursive hostility. Response: targeted disruption. Archive the present, annotate the past. Edit the future."

As she spoke, the Mark changed—segments cracking, reshuffling, becoming less a chain and more a script. Each word she spoke weakened Carmine's hold; the prophecy lines in the air wavered, losing shape, splintering into footnotes and marginalia.

Carmine howled, advancing on Vincent with the word-blade raised. Vincent caught the blade in both hands, ignoring the way it bit into his palms, and wrenched it aside. With a final surge, he head-butted Carmine square in the nose, then drove the ledger down onto the altar, pinning it.

"Mrs Barley!" he screamed. "The pen!"

She tossed the fountain pen with lethal accuracy. Vincent caught it and plunged it into the seam of the ledger. The book writhed, shrieked, then exploded in a gout of ink that covered Vincent from head to toe.

Carmine—no, Cassian—sagged, eyes rolling back. The blade dissolved, black words trailing up into the night and away on the breeze.

For a long moment, nothing happened.

Vincent staggered, fell to one knee. He couldn't feel his hands. His clothes were soaked, sticky, pages of the prophecy now glued to his skin. He looked around. Mrs Barley was slumped against the railing, umbrella snapped, breathing hard. Zara hovered over the carnage, her outline flickering with the afterglow of spent energy.

Ren crawled to Vincent's side, her Mark now a soft, sullen blue. "You did it," she whispered, voice shaking.

Vincent grinned, bloody and ink-stained. "Didn't have much choice, did we?"

From the wreckage, a few mortals began to stir, groaning

and rubbing their heads as if waking from the mother of all hangovers. The Modernisers who'd survived were curled in foetal positions, some sobbing, some just staring at the stars, mouths moving in silent, unfinished sentences.

Vincent helped Ren up. Together, they limped across the deck, dodging bodies and splintered furniture, and found Mrs Barley. She was alive, but her suit was ruined—blood, ink, and at least one thumbprint that did not belong to her.

"You all right?" Ren asked.

Mrs Barley nodded. "Never better. I think I dislocated my wrist."

Vincent surveyed the battlefield. "You think that's it? Is Carmine gone?"

Zara floated down beside them, her face unusually grave. "He's never gone. Just rewritten. This was only a draft."

Vincent looked at his hands—still bleeding, still oozing ink. "Then we'd better sharpen our pencils."

Ren shivered, but her Mark was steady now. She glanced at Vincent, then at Mrs Barley, then at Zara. "If he comes back, we'll be ready."

Mrs Barley managed a smile, then pulled a cigarette from somewhere in her ruined jacket. "We'll put it in the minutes," she said, and lit up with a trembling hand.

Vincent stared at the city, at the blue lights gathering on the street below, at the way the smoke from Mrs Barley's cigarette twisted up into the darkness and disappeared.

He thought of Carmine, of the prophecy, of the next move in the endless game.

And for once, he didn't feel like a victim. He felt like a survivor.

They gathered themselves, patched their wounds, and prepared to write the next chapter—however many drafts it took.

Above them, the night vibrated with new words, waiting to be written.

And in the distance, the first sirens finally began to wail.

EIGHTEEN

In the Council's chamber, rows of tiered benches rose in concentric arcs, each seat occupied by a figure whose suit or gown seemed tailored not merely to the body, but to the soul of its wearer: rich brocades, severe cashmeres, the occasional glint of a signet ring so old it might have witnessed the Black Death in real time. Dark wood panelling stretched up the walls, each panel carved with the names of failed Compacts and forgotten Peaces; the upper reaches vanished into an artificial dusk, where candle chandeliers smouldered like circling predators.

Vincent stood at the centre of the floor with Mrs Barley and Ren at his flanks, each of them caged behind a rail that had no apparent function except to remind the accused how very, very alone they were. Even the air felt different—filtered through some eldritch process that stripped out comfort and replaced it with a low-grade, tooth-tingling static.

At the head of the chamber, seated in a chair that out-throned every throne Vincent had seen outside the Vatican, Elder Mortimer Blackthorn presided. Blackthorn did not so much speak as detonate syllables. He began proceedings with a bang—literally, as his gavel hit the marble dais and left a visible divot.

"Let the record show," Blackthorn intoned, "that the so-called Marked Three have failed in every respect to contain the recursion outbreak. Let the record further show that, in the course of their incompetence, they have rendered the city's human authorities suspicious, compromised the Compact, and —" He flicked his gaze down at a tablet, scrolling with the contemptuous speed of someone deleting spam—"enabled social media to turn a confidential disaster into an international joke."

A ripple of derisive laughter broke out from the Council benches. Vincent caught the eye of Elder Cosgrove, a wolf-faced remnant of the Victorian civil service, whose expression said everything that needed saying about new money and lower breeds. Cosgrove leaned to his neighbour and whispered loudly enough for the chamber to catch: "At this point, even the tabloids are more discreet."

Ren shifted on her feet, the Mark pulsing through her sleeve with a subtle, traitorous glow. Vincent glanced at her, tried to signal "keep your head down," but she was busy fighting the twin battles of fatigue and terror. Her skin had the transparency of cheap rice paper; her jaw was set so tight it looked like it might snap.

Blackthorn continued, "We are now the subject of open ridicule. Mortals are posting your faces, your names—" his eyes bored into Vincent, who returned the stare with an insolence refined over centuries—"alongside images of the revenants and the so-called 'Moderniser Massacre.' Hashtag: Vampires Are Real. Hashtag: Drink Responsibly. Hashtag: Lupo the Livid, trending in four countries." The gavel struck again. "Explain yourselves."

Vincent, for his part, had given up on explanations somewhere between the first and second world wars. He opened his mouth, but Mrs Barley cut in with the lethal efficiency of a bullet train. "Councillors," she said, voice pitched to slice rather than carry. "We have prepared a full incident report, complete with corroborating documentation—eyewitness accounts, electronic forensics, and physical evidence of the Mark's mutation. If the chamber will permit—"

Cosgrove groaned. "Another dossier? Is there a single sentence in it you didn't plagiarise from the previous one?"

Mrs Barley produced a manila envelope thick with ink and stubbornness, handing it to the bailiff (who, Vincent noted, wore gloves as if the envelope might bite). "Appendix B contains *new* photographic evidence of the spectral manifestation at Zara Delacourt's flat. Appendix D includes time-lapse video of the Mark's progression. In sum, we believe Carmine's recursion has evolved beyond simple memetic transmission. He is now—"

Blackthorn cut her off with a raised palm. "You mean to say the ghost is eating its way through the Marked, and you allowed one of your own team—" he jerked his chin at Ren—"to become a vector for this contagion?"

Mrs Barley's face did not move. "We followed Council protocol. Observation, containment, and—when possible—quarantine of infected parties. The failure was not in our methods, but in the underestimation of Carmine's capacity for narrative self-modification."

A chortle from the benches, this time from the rightmost tier, where the youngest Councillors sat like well-fed barristers at a disciplinary tribunal. One, whose accent suggested three generations of Swiss finishing school and a fourth of Alpine inbreeding, said, "Is this the same Carmine who was erased by Council action in 1983? The one who, I was assured, could never again cross the Veil?"

Mrs Barley's hands twitched at her sides, the barest sliver of anger slicing through her composure. "Carmine's deletion was incomplete. Or, more precisely, it was not deletion at all. He was archived."

Vincent admired the way she said it, as if being archived was a fate worse than being shot, buried, and exhumed for a government inquiry.

"Your evidence is circumstantial," Cosgrove sneered. "Spectral photos, corrupted notebooks, hearsay from mortals and that —" he waved vaguely at Ren, "—that barely sentient Marked girl who, by all accounts, spent half the operation unconscious. There is not a single credible witness."

"She's right here," Vincent said, voice cutting through the laughter. "If you want a statement, ask her yourself."

Blackthorn's eyebrows rose, then crashed back down. "Very well. *Miss Ren*, how do you respond to the charge that you are compromised?"

Ren's voice, when it came, was weak but sharp enough to hurt. "The only thing compromised here is the Council's sense of urgency. Carmine isn't just in the Mark, he's using it as a seed crystal. The more you try to erase him, the stronger he gets."

A few Councillors actually leaned forward at that, as if

suddenly aware they might be in the room with the next big disaster.

Mrs Barley seized the moment. "We request immediate resources—personnel, archives, unrestricted network access. If we are to sever the recursion, we need to disrupt the narrative at the source."

Blackthorn regarded them as one might regard a vendor of counterfeit handbags. "Your request is denied. The Council will not expend further resources on an operation led by proven incompetents. The mess is yours to resolve. The consequences, also yours."

He jabbed the gavel for punctuation.

The rest of the Council seemed to relish the moment. Cosgrove actually clapped, twice. Another Councillor, whose face looked like it had been sculpted out of pig iron and old grudges, smiled. "I move that we formally disavow any knowledge of the Lupo team's actions, past, present, or future."

"Seconded," said the Swiss.

Blackthorn surveyed the room. "All in favour—"

A tidal wave of aye's crashed through the chamber. The minority who objected did so in silence.

Vincent raised his hand, waited for Blackthorn's notice. "Just to clarify," he said, "if and when Carmine eats the entire history of London, who gets to write the Council's obituary?"

Blackthorn's eyes narrowed, but he said nothing.

"Just want to make sure the paperwork's in order," Vincent finished, "before we're all replaced by sentient LinkedIn profiles."

Mrs Barley's lips twitched—the nearest she ever came to a smile.

The Council's verdict was as final as it was unoriginal: "You will end this, Lupo, or you will end."

The gavel slammed down, and the lights in the chamber guttered, then blazed with all the subtlety of a firing squad's last request.

Vincent, Ren, and Mrs Barley were escorted out through the lower corridor, passing the chamber's stained-glass windows and the endless gallery of Council martyrs and fuck-ups. The doors closed behind them with the sound of a promise kept for the last time.

They stood in the antechamber for a long, silent minute.

Mrs Barley was the first to break it. "We are, as the mortals say, absolutely fucked."

Vincent grinned, flashing just enough fang to scare a statue. "If you're going to get fired, you might as well burn the building on your way out."

Ren, whose legs looked ready to collapse, muttered, "What now?"

Mrs Barley checked her watch, then her notebook, then Vincent. "Now? We go to ground. We find Carmine's next move before he makes it. And we document everything, because the only thing more dangerous than a prophecy is what happens when no one's left to record it."

Vincent offered Ren his arm. She took it, her grip surprisingly strong. Together, they walked out of the Council building and into the city that, for the first time in a millennium, seemed to have genuinely run out of excuses.

Behind them, in the dark, the chamber's lights flickered one last time, as if the building itself had just been put on notice.

The kitchen at Vincent's flat was not technically an afterlife, but it did a fair impersonation: unlovely light, persistent chill, a pervading sense of unfinished business. The place was thick with old-linoleum ennui and the scent of disinfectant that never quite masked the previous century's worth of spills, leaks, and emotional bleed-through. The table was set for three but laid out for war: coffee mugs half-full, a battered first-aid kit leaking tape and guilt, and the communal laptop open to a spreadsheet headed "Active Containments: FUBAR Edition."

Ren hunched at the head of the table, skin pallid in the lamp's anaemic glow. The blood on her sleeve had darkened to the brown of cheap gravy, but the wound underneath still seeped an ugly purple around the edges. Vincent, who had acquired a meditative expertise in triage, pressed a napkin to the cut and ignored her hiss of pain.

"I said I'm fine," Ren snapped, though her voice quivered and she didn't quite meet his eyes.

Vincent snorted. "You're about as fine as the Moderniser who tried to eat a disco ball. Your pulse is a punchline."

She tried to jerk her hand away, but he held on, dabbing methodically. The room was quiet enough to hear the ticking of the fridge compressor—a clock counting down to something unpleasant.

At the far end, Mrs Barley had set up a command post, filling the air with the arrhythmic percussion of her fountain pen. She made notes in the margins of a printout so heavily annotated it was unclear whether the original text survived.

When she spoke, it was with the absolute finality of a judge handing down the last sentence before retirement.

"The Council has hung us out to dry," she said, not looking up. "Their hope, such as it is, is that we die quickly and take the problem with us."

Vincent tossed the bloody napkin in the general direction of the bin, missed by a wide margin, and watched as Ren cradled her arm. "So, business as usual," he said, but the bitterness was real.

Mrs Barley's pen paused. "Not quite. They're using us as bait. If Carmine's network has a weakness, it's that it can't resist trying to finish the story. We are, at present, the only plausible ending."

A noise overhead—a low, staticky hum—signalled Zara's arrival. She materialised near the ceiling, arms folded like a particularly judgmental house cat. "If you want my advice—" she began.

"No one does," Vincent and Mrs Barley said in near-unison.

She grinned, letting her outline blur at the edges. "Then I'll keep it short. Carmine's not just in the recursion. He is the recursion. We know that every time someone reports, documents, or even thinks about him, it just feeds the damn thing. The council wants us to kill the narrative, but they don't know how to operate without one."

Ren looked up, eyes black in the lamplight. "What do we do? Ignore it and hope it gets bored?"

Zara laughed, a noise that made the bulb flicker. "You're thinking like a librarian. No, you break it. You make it so contradictory, so self-defeating, that even Carmine can't edit his way out."

Vincent felt the tension rise off Mrs Barley like steam. "That's a beautiful theory," he said. "But Carmine's already outmanoeuvred us at every turn. The Mark's spreading, the Modernisers are back online, and the Council's just waiting for the obituary to write itself."

Mrs Barley shut her notebook with a sound like a bear trap. "Then we get ahead of him. We go off-script."

Ren's voice, small but insistent: "We still have the Mark. He can't complete the recursion if he can't close the loop. Right?"

Zara floated lower, ghost-blue and smirking. "It's not about closing the loop. It's about who gets to write the next line. That's you, darling. Always was."

For a moment, no one spoke. Vincent paced to the sink, filled a glass, and drank it in one unbroken swallow. He stared out the window, watching the streetlights paint the alleyway with the half-life of failed ambition.

He turned, braced both hands on the counter, and faced the team.

"No more stakeouts. No more forms. We do this on our terms. We break the loop, even if we have to snap it over our own necks."

Mrs Barley nodded, no trace of doubt in her eyes. "Agreed."

Ren managed a smile, shaky but defiant. "Let's write something he can't predict."

Zara clapped, silent and insincere. "Break a leg, kids. Or a Mark."

Vincent exhaled, feeling the chill settle into his bones. "First things first," he said, looking at Ren's wound, then at the wall where, just visible in the lamplight, a new line of Carmine's script crawled up from the skirting board.

He smiled. "Let's see how Carmine likes being edited by a smutty paranormal romance writer."

The flat, for one long moment, held its breath. And then, with a click and a thrum, the city outside beckoned—ready for a new draft, written in their blood, sweat, and very questionable sense of teamwork.

NINETEEN

The Moderniser HQ had been assembled with all the subtlety of a neurodivergent toddler at a glitter sale. The "loft apartment" (according to the listing; in truth, a repurposed former carpet warehouse with more Building Regulation violations than lease amendments) was a delirious spectacle of taste, money, and unapologetic solipsism. The exposed brick walls, already a cliché by 2007, had been sandblasted and re-exposed until their only remaining function was as a backdrop for the riot of neon vampire signage. Professional ring lights stood at rigid attention like stormtroopers, each optimised for a different influencer skin tone, while ceiling-mounted cameras tracked the floor space in slow, algorithmic arcs. Even the furniture—the oblong divans, the surgically white kitchen counter, the beanbag chairs that looked like enormous silicone breast implants—had been selected less for utility than for how they'd play on a phone screen.

Vincent wanted to burn the place to the ground. Failing

that, he'd have settled for arson on the branded "Type O-MG Detox Cleanse" display, which took pride of place on an end table beside a vase of genetically unrecognisable flowers.

He took one step inside and was nearly blinded by the confluence of ring-light glare and weaponised pink LED. He bared his teeth, a reflexive act, and watched the ring lights respond by flicking into "fang highlight" mode. Someone had programmed them to accentuate the canines.

Ren entered behind him, hoodie up and hands sunk deep in her pockets. She scanned the open floor with the cautious awe of someone who'd walked into a cult headquarters and was still holding out hope for a reasonable conversation. The Mark on her arm throbbed once, a faint blue through her sleeve, as if echoing her sense of anticlimax.

Mrs Barley brought up the rear, clipboard already deployed, and coat buttoned against the visual assault. She did not so much as flinch at the onslaught of pastel lighting or the three distinct sound systems playing at war with each other. She located the nearest flat surface, cleared it of two unopened "Bite Me, Babe" blood-smoothie cartons, and set up her mobile command post with the economy of someone who had survived eight years in Council procurement and the London Borough of Hackney.

The hosts arrived as a matched set, each more improbable than the last.

Aurelia Voss glided across the open floor, her heels silent on the polished concrete, every inch of her calculated for maximum optical resonance. She had platinum-blonde hair, eyes the colour of zero-calorie blue raspberry, and cheekbones that appeared to have been imported from a climate with fewer human rights laws. Her suit was a single, perfect shade of white, unmarred by even the memory of previous wearers. She extended a hand to Vincent, but the gesture was less "greeting" than "testing to see if he'd refuse it in front of an audience."

Cass Roe followed, juggling three phones on selfie sticks, each already streaming to a different audience. He had the nervous, twitching charm of a gameshow host on day three of a juice fast, and he carried a portable power brick the size of a kilo block of C-4. "Lupo the Lightless in the house!" he announced, beaming directly into his phone. "Let the record show, fam: the OG's arrived. Smash that like button if you want him to bare the fangs."

Trailing at a distance was Nyx Calder, who wore their DJ headphones like a crown of thorns and kept a pair of mirrored sunglasses perched on their nose, despite the fact that the room was now brighter than the average operating theatre. They gave a two-fingered wave, then collapsed onto a beanbag with the resignation of someone expecting to die there.

Vincent surveyed the room, eyes narrowing on the display of "Type O-MG" again. "Do you people ever have an off switch?"

Aurelia flashed a smile that, for a split second, looked almost sincere. "Only if there's a better brand deal in the morning."

"Tell that to your mate here," Vincent said, gesturing at Cass, who had already resumed his monologue.

Cass ignored him, tilting the phone for a slow 360-degree pan of the loft. "Council's finest, right here! Here to drop some existential drama on the Moderniser movement. Hit that follow if you want to see who throws the first punch." He swivelled the camera at Mrs Barley, who did not dignify the provocation with a look.

Vincent's fangs itched. "Turn that off," he said, not even raising his voice. "Before I turn you inside out and sell the highlights to your TikTok rivals."

Cass considered, briefly. "I could do that, yeah." He pocketed one of the phones but kept the main one rolling, now streaming in "stealth" mode. "But then the Council would just edit the footage anyway."

Vincent reached for the phone, hand closing over Cass's wrist with a grip that suggested one of them would be leaving the encounter with less blood than they'd started with.

Aurelia stepped in, voice placid. "We're already trending, Vincent. If you want us to stop, say please."

Vincent bared his teeth, but Mrs Barley beat him to the punch. "Enough," she said, her tone set to "headmistress in the last week of term." She rapped her clipboard against the table, hard enough to puncture the ambient whine of the loft's sound system.

The room, for a fraction of a second, actually went quiet.

Mrs Barley looked at the three Modernisers, eyes cold and unblinking. "I'll be brief. Carmine's recursion is accelerating. His next phase is imminent. If you'd like to avoid being edited out of existence, you'll cooperate with us for the duration of this crisis."

Aurelia's eyes widened, not with surprise, but with something more calculating. "That's a lot of Council talk for someone who's technically in disgrace."

Ren perked up, leaning against the wall. "We're not Council. Not anymore. We're the only ones who know what's coming."

Cass had already started a new stream, this one angled at Ren. "Go on, then. Tell the world. Is it true you had to drink Lupo's blood to survive?"

Ren glared, but Vincent rolled his eyes. "It was a medical procedure, not a bloody OnlyFans exclusive."

Nyx snorted from their beanbag. "Everything's an Only-Fans exclusive if you angle it right."

Mrs Barley took a deep, bracing breath. "We have a proposal," she said, eyes on Aurelia. "You have numbers, we have intel. If we pool our resources, we may stand a chance of disrupting Carmine's chain before he upgrades to the next iteration."

Cass grinned. "You want a collab? We're listening."

Aurelia folded her arms, studying Mrs Barley with a predator's stillness. "Why should we help the Council that spent the last decade trying to erase us?"

Vincent interjected, voice flat. "Because Carmine's not picky. If he wins, you're all canon-fodder. He'll rewrite the lot of you—Council, Modernisers, influencers, even your sponsors."

Nyx shrugged. "I mean, not the worst way to go. At least it's not as boring as being a day-walker drone for Council legal."

Ren stepped forward, the Mark on her arm faintly visible through her sleeve. "You don't get it. If we win, you get respect. Not just likes or clickbait. Actual say in what comes next."

Cass raised his eyebrows, genuinely intrigued. "And if you lose?"

Mrs Barley didn't blink. "You'll never know. Because you won't be there to post about it."

There was a moment—a real, uncurated pause—where even Aurelia looked uncertain.

Vincent seized it. "Look," he said, voice all gravel and exhaustion. "We didn't come here to guilt-trip you. You want to be legends? Fine. But this is the last prophecy anyone's going to remember. You in, or not?"

Aurelia pursed her lips, fingers drumming against the neon-lit table. "You drive a hard bargain, Lupo. But you're right. No one survives a rewrite unless they're the one holding the pen."

She extended her hand again, this time toward Mrs Barley.

Mrs Barley took it, her grip like a steel cable.

Cass whooped. "Hell yes! Time to go viral for real."

Nyx, still horizontal, just said, "Cool. Someone wake me when Carmine arrives."

Vincent exhaled, the tension in his shoulders dropping half a centimetre. He eyed the "Type O-MG" poster one last time and considered, briefly, whether it would be cathartic to set it on fire.

Ren nudged him, quietly. "You all right?"

Vincent smirked. "Never better."

Across the room, Cass had already updated the group chat. The city was watching, and for the first time, Vincent hoped maybe that was a good thing.

But as the Modernisers closed ranks and Mrs Barley began outlining the plan on her clipboard, Vincent felt the old dread, the one that said nothing this easy ever ended well.

The neon signs flickered, ring lights humming, and somewhere in the chaos, a fresh line of prophecy began to write itself —in hashtags, in blood, in the pulse behind his eyes.

TWENTY

Vincent's flat had become a waiting room for the world's most anxious disaster. Vincent sat at the chipped breakfast bar with his hands wrapped round a mug of yesterday's coffee, now reheated to the point of active spite.

Ren paced the flat, making five-step circuits between the window and the kitchen door, her battered trainers squeaking in counterpoint to the living room lamp's electrical death rattle. The Mark on her forearm pulsed with a lurid, anaemic blue, the outline just visible through the cotton of her jumper. She kept glancing at her phone as though expecting an update on their odds of survival, but the only messages were from Mrs Barley, texting her on running commentary from across the room.

Zara herself floated in the half-lit gloom, her form growing less attached to the world with every minute. She hovered a good foot off the ground, shoes trailing an after-image, hair fanned around her head like the world's most anhedonic halo. Each time the lamp flickered, Zara seemed to lose a degree of opacity, until it looked as if her bones might simply collapse into a drift of blue-white dust.

She regarded the group with a clinical detachment that Vincent recognised as pre-emptive nostalgia: nostalgia for a reality about to be overwritten, or for the selves they would be leaving behind.

"Right," she said, voice splitting at the edges. "You all ready for the house special?"

Vincent sipped his coffee. "Does it come with chips?"

Ren, who had been chewing her lip to ribbons, stopped pacing. "Just tell us if this is going to kill us."

Zara's eyes glinted, phosphorescent and unkind. "Probably not all of you at once."

Mrs Barley, pen poised, did not look up. "Proceed, please."

Zara raised both hands and, with a gesture that belonged at the climax of a Victorian séance, gathered the room's shadows toward her like a drawstring bag. The lightshade overhead shuddered, then stilled, its light drawn into a singularity above Zara's open palms. The shadows pooled, eddied, and then—at a wordless signal—exploded out again, sweeping through the flat and peeling the surface off everything they touched.

Words began to slough off the wallpaper in long, glutinous strips. Letters bubbled up from the paint, curled into themselves, then dropped to the floor with the sound of wet leaves. On the counter, the branding from a Tesco carrier bag inverted, so that "Every Little Helps" read as an accusation instead of a slogan. Even the labels on Mrs Barley's highlighters began to run, forming little rainbow deltas of unresolved language.

Vincent felt his teeth begin to itch.

Zara's voice dropped into a register that set the glassware

rattling. "Here's the pitch: Carmine's not in the world. He's in the draft of the world. The bit underneath—the version they tried to cross out. To reach him, we have to slip through the margin. That means finding the seam."

Ren swallowed, her hand pressed to the Mark as if it might bolt off her arm and start a new life somewhere warmer. "You mean like a... a fold in the universe?"

"More like a bad edit," said Zara. "There's no clean break. Just a tear, and hope you don't snag on the way through."

Mrs Barley scribbled furiously, muttering, "Subject explains metaphysical incursion as function of incomplete erasure. Hypothesis: Carmine occupies the interstitial spaces between iterations."

Vincent pushed his mug aside. "I always hated libraries."

Zara grinned, though it looked like it cost her. "Good news, then. This one doesn't carry any of your books, and I don't think they're too fussed about making noise."

The lamp burst, showering the room in shards. The light from Zara's hands was now the only illumination: twin vortexes of cold fire, spiralling out and meeting in front of her like two threads winding a new rope. As she focused, the strips of word-flesh on the wallpaper curled back, revealing a growing void, the edges of which pulsed with the sickly phosphorescence of a glow stick fished from the Thames.

Ren's Mark surged, sending tendrils of light up her wrist and into the palm of her hand. She stared at it, then at the wall, her face pale and set. The air between her and the rift felt viscous, like the bit of a nightmare where you have to run but your legs are moving through syrup.

Mrs Barley finished her note, snapped the pad shut, and

addressed the void with the same tone she used for parking wardens and loan officers. "Please describe the parameters of passage, Miss Delacourt. Is the effect continuous, or must we traverse in sequence?"

"Just go when you're ready," said Zara, who by now was only a face, hair, and hands. "I'll keep the gate open as long as I can. But it's going to hurt."

Vincent rose, dusted glass from his lap, and squared his shoulders. "First time for everything," he muttered.

Ren stepped forward, but the Mark did the rest: her hand, guided by some editorial muscle memory, reached into the wound in the wall. The moment her fingers touched the other side, her body jerked as if shocked. The Mark glowed blue to white, then pure blinding, drawing the outline of her bones through her skin like an X-ray in a power cut.

She didn't scream. Instead, she turned to the others and said, "It's like... being read from behind your own eyes."

Vincent took her other hand, steadying her. Mrs Barley, never one to cede control of an experiment, walked in last, notepad in one hand and a highlighter in the other, already annotating the experience.

The rift widened, and for a moment, the world on the other side bled through: endless shelves, rising into darkness, books and binders and ledgers stitched together with wire and sinew, their spines twitching as if eager for new content. The air was thick with the sound of turning pages, but each page turned itself, as if afraid to linger too long on a single moment.

Vincent stared into the rift and felt something old and unwelcome stir in his chest.

"I really hate libraries," he repeated, and together they

stepped through, the words of their world peeling off and fluttering after them like moths.

Behind them, Zara's voice echoed: "Remember—don't look back. If you do, the edit never lets go."

The rift closed, swallowing the light and the sound, and for a moment, Vincent's flat returned to its old, haunted stillness.

Only the floor, now covered in a fine mulch of letters and punctuation, suggested that anything had ever happened at all.

The world on the other side of the rift was a library, if libraries could be constructed entirely out of existential dread and the kind of architectural ambitions that usually resulted in criminal charges, or a Channel 4 documentary.

Shelves towered, vanished into black mist above, only to reappear hundreds of feet later, bridging gaps with rickety spiral walkways made of bent iron brackets and threadbare citation tape. The stacks curved and branched in fractal patterns, each receding line of shelving inscribed with errata, bloodstains, and the untranslatable margin notes of a hundred lost scribes. Somewhere, high overhead, a drip of ink fell—slow as death, fat as a raindrop—and splattered on the floor at Vincent's feet, where it immediately began to sizzle and spread, dissolving a knot of loose footnotes that had been skittering across the flagstones like silverfish.

Ren stumbled as she landed, nearly faceplanting on a carpet of discarded index cards. The Mark on her arm pulsed, each beat radiating through her entire body like a second, less reliable circulatory system. She clenched her teeth and blinked until the afterimages faded. The sensation of being watched—by the books, by the footnotes, by the invisible recorders lurking in the shadows—was overwhelming.

Mrs Barley arrived last, notepad still at the ready. She surveyed the stacks with professional disdain, already scanning for exits, choke points, or, failing that, the nearest safe desk from which to monitor and judge.

The Modernisers came through in a clump, led by Aurelia and flanked by Cass and Nyx, who each carried two phones and three separate battery packs. The ring lights, which had looked faintly ridiculous in the living world, now burned with a blue-white heat that cast more shadow than illumination. Every so often, a shadow detached from the rest and scuttled up a bookshelf, where it hid in the index and pretended it was not afraid.

Zara coalesced in the centre of the group, less a body now than a negative-space halo. "Welcome to the Archive Between Pages," she announced, and her voice echoed in the stacks with the force of a prophecy delivered over a cheap supermarket PA system. "Population: currently us, and whatever Carmine has rustled up."

Vincent flexed his jaw. His fangs ached, as if reacting to some deep, sourceless hunger in the stacks. The urge to tear into something—book, person, himself—was strong, and for once he didn't trust his own instincts. He looked at the nearest shelf, where a single volume with his name on the spine throbbed faintly in time with the Mark on Ren's arm.

Zara glided ahead, pausing only to warn, "Don't read aloud. Everything here wants to be written again."

Cass immediately pointed his phone at the shelves. "What happens if we livestream?"

Mrs Barley barked, "It'll make a copy of you so accurate, even your mother wouldn't know the difference." She glared at the phone as if it was personally responsible for the decline of Western civilisation.

Aurelia, unbothered, took a selfie with the nearest shelf, duck lips poised, and captioned it "#AfterlifeVibes." The shelf responded by emitting a low, disapproving growl.

Ren shivered and pulled her hoodie tighter, but the Mark was now so bright it illuminated the inside of her sleeve. "Which way?" she asked, voice barely more than a suggestion.

Zara, who had by now developed the presence of a weather system, led them deeper into the stacks. Each corridor twisted, then doubled back, then split into three or five or eleven alternate realities, only for the paths to reconverge a few seconds later. Occasionally, a shelf would collapse and reassemble itself on the other side of the corridor, but only when no one was looking directly at it.

As they moved, the stacks came alive. Books stretched out their covers, fluttering pages like wings. Some drifted free, riding the air in slow, predatory loops. A dictionary the size of a labrador slithered along the ground, chasing the footnotes and devouring any that wandered too far from the pack.

Vincent watched it all in silence, his usual snark running up against the limits of language. Even for him, the Archive was a little much.

Ren's steps faltered as the Mark yanked her to the left, down a staircase made entirely out of torn disciplinary forms and bound together with Council-grade red tape. At the bottom, the air changed: colder, denser, like the inside of a bank vault or the brief hush after a bomb threat.

They gathered on a landing that overlooked the rest of the Archive. It went on for miles. Possibly forever. The geometry fought itself, every angle an impossible number, every corridor longer than the building it was in.

Zara stopped at the balustrade, flickered into half a dozen different outlines, then stilled. "He's close," she said. "He's always been close. He never really left."

There was a noise—like a page being torn, but loud enough to vibrate the teeth. The far end of the corridor split open. Out stepped Carmine.

He wore a suit three centuries out of date, but it had aged perfectly. His eyes, when they caught Vincent's, were the same: clever, hungry, faintly amused by everyone else's ineptitude. He had the air of a man who had never once been surprised by anything, except maybe his own capacity for self-destruction.

"Welcome," said Carmine, and it was like being handed an eviction notice for one's soul. "You've made a mess of the outside. I thought I'd tidy up in here."

Vincent stepped forward, Mrs Barley and Ren at his sides. The Modernisers clustered behind, their ring lights flickering.

Carmine inclined his head. "You brought friends. And the Mark. Very good. I always said you needed an audience, Lupo."

Vincent grinned, though the skin around his mouth barely moved. "Wouldn't want you to miss your own closing night."

Carmine's eyes crinkled at the edges. "Oh, there's no closing. Only the next edition."

He looked at Ren, then at Mrs Barley, then at the

Modernisers. "You think you can overwrite me? By all means—try."

The stacks began to close in, shelves sliding on invisible rails, forming a ring around the confrontation. The books leaned in, eager to see the outcome. Even the footnotes stopped moving, clustered at the margins.

Zara floated above, voice now a whisper that echoed from every surface. "He's bound to the narrative. If you can break his story, you can end him. But you have to mean it."

Mrs Barley drew her pen, clicked it twice. "Ready?"

Ren's Mark was so bright it burned shadows into her face. "Ready."

Vincent bared his fangs. For once, it felt good.

Carmine's smile did not falter, but the shadow behind him stretched, growing larger, darker, until it filled the entire corridor.

"After you, Vincent," said Carmine. "I insist."

Vincent stepped into the ring, the Archive humming in anticipation.

"Let's edit, then," he said. And the battle began.

TWENTY-ONE

The Archive responded to violence with violence. At Vincent's words, the air split with a percussive crack and the nearest shelves collapsed inwards, spines flexing as if to defend the secrets within. Dust and shredded index cards fountained into the aisle, and, somewhere in the gloom overhead, a vast flock of loose pages unbound themselves from their volumes, twisting and wheeling in sick geometric shoals. The stack corridor where Carmine stood shuddered as if struck by a train of lawyers.

Vincent braced for the first rush, expecting Carmine to attack—old habits, hard to break—but the apparition merely smiled and beckoned, and the real threat came from the Archive itself. The floor pitched, the shelves on either side reconfiguring into a new angle of attack. He heard Mrs Barley's heels scrabble for traction as the ground shifted to a thirty-degree incline.

"A little warning next time, please," she gritted, clutching the balustrade with all of her strength.

"Consider this the evacuation drill," Vincent shot back. "Follow me, or stay for the sequel."

He launched forward, foot skidding on a drift of sticky errata. The path ahead wasn't a path anymore—it was a corridor one moment, a spiral ramp the next, then a funhouse chute lined with books that snapped at ankles like starving dogs. Every few feet, the stacks exploded sideways, ejecting tomes and binders in a hail of paper and bureaucracy.

Somewhere to the left, Vincent heard the Modernisers shrieking; Cass and Nyx barrelled past, ducking a fusillade of desk calendars sharpened to a knifepoint. Aurelia followed, radiant and furious, batting aside a swooping flock of Banned Accountancy Practices.

Vincent's headlong charge slowed as he realised Ren wasn't behind him. He spun, just in time to see her stumble, clutching at her arm. The Mark had changed colour, not blue but a sulphuric white, leaking streams of light with every pulse. She looked up, face blank, and took a step away from him—no, not away. Toward the epicentre.

"Ren!" Vincent barked.

She blinked, eyelids flickering with afterimages, and made a noise halfway between a cough and a sob. "He's... it's calling me. Like a fire alarm in my head."

Mrs Barley reached her first, hands steady, but Ren's legs gave out and she dropped, one knee buckling. The Mark blazed. A ring of incunabula tore itself from the shelf above, circled her head, and then snapped shut, forming a crown of densely printed pages.

Vincent dived, heedless, and caught her by the wrist just as a river of ink broke through the baseboards, swirling round her ankles. The liquid was alive: not metaphorically, but literally, words squirming through it like lampreys. They lapped at Ren's shoes, then surged upward, wrapping her shins in a writhing sentence.

Vincent dug in, yanking her free with a growl. "Not today," he said, fangs half-extended with the stress. The Mark fought him, white fire up her arm, but he ground it out by sheer brute force and a lifetime's practice at refusing to be anyone's test subject.

Mrs Barley, pragmatic to the last, snapped her notebook open and began dictating at the ink river. "Subject displays aggressive narrative tension. Suggest immediate de-escalation via redirection—"

The ink, insulted by the attempt at psychoanalysis, recoiled and spat a spray of black across her skirt, then retreated under the shelves, hissing.

Vincent staggered upright, Ren draped across his arms and blinking. Her skin was hot to the touch—unusual, for her—but her eyes tracked, at least.

"Snap out of it," he said. "You're not a library card."

She managed a weak grin. "He's using me as a bookmark. That's new."

Above, the sky—or the suggestion of a sky—shivered. Pages rained down, each one screaming. At first, Vincent thought it was just the wind, but as the paper shredded itself against the stacks, the voices became distinct: snatches of dialogue, clipped sentences, howled footnotes and the echo of a thousand forgotten memos. It was a swarm of abandoned stories, their words competing for the chance to overwrite what came next.

"Can we get a move on?" Cass yelled from the next aisle

over. "The phone battery's down to six percent and my backup powerbank just tried to murder me."

Aurelia, unruffled, dispatched a quartet of flying ledgers with a backhanded swipe. "He's stalling us. Carmine wants the Mark to finish rewriting before we can stop it."

Nyx, trailing, called out, "Heads up!" and a cluster of ghostly figures materialised in the intersection.

The revenants were worse than Vincent remembered. In the world of flesh and mortgage, a revenant was a dull, predatory thing—tough to kill, but ultimately killable, its mind a patchwork of regret and rat poison. Here, in the Archive, they were nightmare bureaucrats, constructed from the detritus of failed drafts: limbs stitched together from columns of text, faces a patchwork of legal precedent and condemnation, eyes deep wells of italicised yearning. They glowed with a sickly halo, as if radioactive from centuries of exposure to other people's failures.

The leading revenant, a composite of outdated bylaws and shredded parliamentary minutes, lurched at Mrs Barley. It opened its mouth, and a flood of redacted sentences spilled out: "Subsection. Paragraph. Clause. You are not the intended recipient. Return to sender. Return to sender—"

Mrs Barley sidestepped the swipe with the ease of a seasoned London Underground commuter, then jammed her fountain pen into the revenant's eye. Ink jetted out in a plume, and the thing staggered, voice modulating to a static whine. She withdrew the pen with a flourish and scrawled a line across the revenant's chest, where it sizzled and began to unravel, the words of its body detaching and floating up like bad Amazon reviews.

"Nice," Vincent said. "Do that a few hundred more times and we'll be home in time for tea."

Mrs Barley didn't dignify it with a response, already searching the shelves for anything else that could be weaponised.

The next revenant was faster: an amalgam of police reports and social media threads, its hands serrated with stapler wire. It went for Ren, who had managed to prop herself against a shelf, but Vincent blocked it, fangs now fully out. He parried the stapler hand with his forearm, ignoring the pain, and slammed his heel through the revenant's knee. The joint snapped, and the thing buckled, but instead of going down it regenerated— pages and thread closing the wound in real time.

It was, Vincent realised, never going to run out of material.

He yelled, "Zara! Any time you want to rewrite the odds—"

A voice, everywhere and nowhere, replied: "You always did have a flair for the dramatic, Lupo." Zara's outline glitched into being at the head of the aisle, blue corona spiking. She swept her hands wide, and a gust of spectral cold tore through the stacks, freezing every page midair. The raining stories stopped. The air filled with the shudder of ice and possibility.

Zara, more energy than form now, grinned at the team. "You get two minutes. Make them count."

Vincent didn't wait for debate. "Down the ramp," he ordered. "He wants the Mark, but he won't risk destroying it. That's our lever."

Mrs Barley hoisted Ren with zero ceremony, slinging her over one shoulder like a misbehaving houseplant. Together, the trio skidded down the ramp, ducking a final flurry of footnotes as the Archive rearranged the corridor behind them. The revenants, momentarily baffled by the loss of narrative gravity, staggered after, but the shelf walls closed with a thunderclap, cutting them off.

Ahead, the corridor opened into a vault. There was no other word for it—walls, ceiling, floor, all fused into one continuous curve of shelving, every inch lined with Carmine's output. At the centre, illuminated by the dying light of the Mark, stood a single desk, upon which rested a manuscript: the original draft, bound in chain and wax, leaking a pale blue mist that smelled of nothing but endings.

Vincent slowed, careful. "That's the kill switch," he said. "Or the detonator. Or both."

Ren, propped against the door, gasped, "If we touch it, does it end? Or start over?"

Mrs Barley's eyes gleamed, the prospect of a solution reanimating every line in her face. "We don't touch it. We annotate."

Vincent smirked. "You want to edit Carmine?"

She squared her shoulders. "No. I want to footnote him to death."

For a second, even Vincent had to respect the plan. He handed her his pen.

Mrs Barley approached the desk. Every step was a risk; the air grew heavier, the words on the walls bristling as if to intervene. But she pressed on, and took a seat at the desk. The Mark on Ren's arm began to pulse in time with the page turns, softer now, but still inexorable.

Vincent stood guard, eyes flicking between the entrance and the shelves, half-expecting Carmine to materialise and tip the desk over. He'd almost prefer that to the suspense.

Behind them, the rest of the Modernisers tumbled into the

vault, battered but alive. Cass immediately started livestreaming, Nyx ducked behind a reading chair, and Aurelia—ever the tactician—scanned the scene for a better angle.

At the desk, Mrs Barley paused. "Ready?" she asked, not looking back.

Vincent glanced at Ren. She nodded, lips tight. "Do it."

Mrs Barley uncapped the pen and, with the calculated grace of a hangman, began to annotate the manuscript. Each footnote burned into the paper, flaring blue then fading to ash. The text fought back—lines of prophecy slithering to the edge, trying to overwrite her comments—but she was relentless, carving citation after citation until the manuscript itself began to smoulder.

A scream echoed through the Archive. The shelves convulsed, ejecting books in all directions. The desk rattled, the chains clattering against the wood, and the air went cold enough to crack teeth.

At the entrance, the revenants gathered, blocked by a wall of fresh annotations. They banged at the invisible barrier, howling, but every time Mrs Barley added a new footnote, one of them evaporated into a fine mist of unreferenced misery.

Vincent watched, fascinated and horrified, as Carmine's voice emerged from the stack, stretched thin and desperate: "You can't kill a story. Not while anyone remembers."

Mrs Barley pressed the pen to the final page. "But you can edit it," she said. "And you are not the author anymore."

With a final stroke, she signed her name.

The Archive convulsed. The light in the vault snapped to white, then black, then an impossible colour Vincent's eyes refused to process. The desk exploded, manuscript incinerated in a nova of blue fire. The Mark on Ren's arm snapped—clean, bloodless, and final.

For a moment, there was no sound at all.

Then, slowly, the Archive began to fill with the quiet shuffle of pages settling into place.

Vincent let out a breath he hadn't known he was holding.

Mrs Barley turned, pen still smoking, and offered a faint, exhausted smile. "It's done," she said.

Ren slumped, half-laughing, half-crying. The Mark on her skin was gone, replaced by a single, elegant scar: a footnote, nothing more.

Vincent reached for words, found only the old ones. "Next time," he said, "we're burning the library."

Cass, already uploading the final moments, nodded. "Yeah, but first—can we get out? I think my phone's haunted."

The Archive, now benign, opened a path.

And together, battered but whole, they followed it toward the exit—leaving behind only the echoes, and the ashes, of a story that had finally run out of versions.

They nearly made it to the exit before the Archive rebelled, one last time, against closure.

Vincent heard it first—a seismic rustle, like a stadium of legal pads being turned at once. The chill hit next, cold enough to sting the teeth and slow the heart. The corridor behind them swelled, impossible geometry bulging from the walls, the curve of shelving stretching to accommodate a figure far larger than any human, or even the sum of all the humans who'd ever tried to document the supernatural.

Carmine arrived in the manner of a virus that had given up on subtlety. The walls strained and then split, vomiting out a composite of flesh and footnotes. The body was almost Vincent's height, but wreathed in a corona of burning, recombining words; the skin flickered between pallor and newsprint, each muscle group annotated in a Latin no longer spoken by mortals. Carmine's face was a revolving glitch—sometimes the arch nose and hungry lips Vincent remembered, more often a tangle of headline, paragraph, and the odd meme-worthy jpeg spliced in for narrative effect.

He smiled, and the teeth were punctuation marks, every one of them sharp.

"Not so fast," said Carmine, and his voice hit like a speaker system installed in a concrete bunker—loud enough to set the air vibrating, overlaid with several secondary voices, each one disagreeing with the one before.

Vincent drew up short, angling his body to block Ren and Mrs Barley from the point of impact. The Mark on Ren's arm, newly scarred and non-functional, sizzled faintly in the cold, but she held steady, watching Carmine with the same rapt horror one might afford a collapse in a condemned stadium.

Mrs Barley set her jaw and closed her notepad, as if unwilling to give Carmine any more source material.

Carmine extended a hand, and the corridor responded: pages ripped from the nearest shelf, flying in tight formation like a murder of crows. They circled, then dove, the leading edges curling into blades sharp enough to split hair or, more to the point, bone.

Vincent let the first page hit, taking it on his forearm. The cut was shallow, but it bled ink, not blood—a reminder that the Archive was making its own rules now. He braced for the next volley, shifting so Mrs Barley could pull Ren to relative safety behind a bookcase labelled "Interminable Disputes: Volume 12".

The Modernisers, less equipped for physical violence, ducked and scattered. Cass was first to recover, swinging his phone at the barrage and hoping his torch and Spotify playlist would keep the horrors at bay. Aurelia, eyes alight, snatched one of the flying endpaper razors from the air and flung it back, scoring a neat line down Carmine's cheek. It healed before her eyes, the wound closing with a crawl of italicised regret.

Carmine laughed. "You see? You edit, I rewrite. That's how this ends, Lupo."

Vincent spat a mouthful of ink onto the carpet. "You always were a lazy plagiarist."

He scanned the battlefield—no, the field of edits. The Archive now bent around Carmine's gravity, each shelf turning to face him, the floor rippling underfoot with a pulse of pure, unfiltered narrative. Vincent didn't need to be a prophet to know the only way forward was through.

He pointed at the nearest hazard—an avalanche of Council minutes, tumbling like rockfall. "Ren, left. Mrs Barley, disrupt the shelf at six o'clock. Cass, if you're going to film, try not to die during the unboxing."

Mrs Barley needed no further instruction. She smashed the base of the stack with a kick, toppling the column of books into the path of a second flock of slicing pages. Cass ducked beneath the chaos, rolling a shoulder and coming up grinning, his phone's battery miraculously unscathed.

Ren, pale but moving, made the left turn, only to skid to a stop as the floor liquefied into a river of black typeface. She nearly went under before Vincent caught her by the collar, hauling her onto a raft of bound journals. The ink river surged, words coiling and writhing, but he kept her above water, knees locked, teeth bared.

Carmine watched, amused. "You should let her go. She'd make a great prologue."

"Piss off," Vincent replied, planting his feet.

Then Carmine attacked in earnest.

The air exploded with pages, lines, and stray comments. Some were sharpened into spears, others into netting that tried to bind Vincent's arms to his sides. He batted away the first, but the second caught his wrist, and he felt the burn of annotation. It wasn't just pain; it was Carmine's voice in his head, rewriting his thoughts, flooding his memory with alternative histories.

Vincent fought it the only way he knew—by refusing to participate.

"Louder, Carmine," he taunted, "maybe this time you'll actually have something to say."

That did it. Carmine stepped forward, his form swelling to fill the corridor, the words on his chest now burning with phosphorescent malice. "You think this is about story? It's about survival, Vincent. No story, no memory. No memory, no self. I didn't come back to watch you turn me into myth."

He lunged, the Archive bending around him in a scream of tortured shelving. Vincent met the attack head-on, letting the fangs come all the way out. He grappled with Carmine, and it was like wrestling a live wire of narrative and venom. Every punch landed with a quotation. Every kick was accompanied by a critique.

"You always take the easy way," Vincent snarled, digging his claws into Carmine's forearm.

Carmine's arm dissolved into script, then re-formed as a python of marginalia. "And you always play the martyr. Maybe try something new, for once."

The fight spilled down the corridor, smashing furniture and walls of text. Pages swarmed Vincent, trying to pinion his limbs, wrap his throat, blind his eyes. He bit them—literally, in some cases—his teeth sinking into pulp and history and the taste of old ink.

Mrs Barley, not content to be a bystander, leveraged her own weapon: she tore pages from the nearest shelf and scribbled new lines over them, then hurled them at Carmine. Each one hit like a truth bomb, burning a hole in his shell. For every wound, Carmine patched with fresh story, but Mrs Barley's edits slowed him, forced him to recalculate.

Ren, clinging to the floor, watched in awe and terror. The Mark, dead a moment ago, now throbbed with a new energy—a relay, feeding Carmine's own power back against him. She pressed her hand to her arm, grit her teeth, and focused on the most important job in the world: staying alive long enough for Vincent to win.

Carmine roared, an inhuman, mechanical sound, and the entire Archive vibrated. The shelves collapsed, then rebuilt themselves in reverse order, books shuffling on their own. A black hole of narrative gravity opened at the far end of the aisle, sucking everything not nailed down toward it.

Vincent felt the drag. It was like being pulled apart at the page. He clung to Carmine, refusing to be dislodged.

"You want the ending?" he gasped. "Fine. We'll write you one."

He wrenched Carmine around and, using the last of his leverage, hurled him onto the dais. They tumbled, a mess of limbs and stories and unresolved plot points, both too weak to deliver the killer blow.

Vincent looked back at Ren and Mrs Barley and then to Aurelia and her influencers and smiled.

"Make him Insta-famous."

TWENTY-TWO

Carmine reeled—caught between corporeal and theoretical, flickering like a dodgy Wi-Fi signal, his face sometimes the old, sly arch-scholar, sometimes a blank patch where nothing had yet been written.

Vincent saw the opening and, battered as he was, did what any apex predator with a decent sense of timing would do: he let the influencers go first.

Aurelia Voss hit the dais in a full runway strut, platinum hair catching the reflection of every ruined ring light as she rallied her crew behind her. Cass was at her side, all hyperventilated adrenaline, holding his phone in both hands as though the device itself had become a religious icon. Behind them, Nyx spun up a soundtrack on their phone—every bass drop matched to the rhythm of the Archive's dying heartbeat.

The Modernisers were not so much a phalanx as a flash-mob: all angles, energy, and immediate, weaponised presence. They moved as one, each pulling a ring light from the pocket of a hoodie, or the sleeve of a crop top, or, in Nyx's case, from the inside of a battered, stickered flight case. The lights went up—blue-white, hellishly bright, some with "whitening" filters, others tuned to a tone so harsh it could have strip-mined the soul from a medium-sized company mascot.

Phones out, cameras up, they advanced in a ripple of performance and planned spontaneity. "Showtime," hissed Aurelia, and it was unclear if she was talking to her team or the watching millions on the other side of her streaming account.

Vincent had the rare pleasure of seeing Carmine—old nemesis, shadow puppeteer, king of the confidential footnote—look genuinely taken aback. The sudden, full-court press of attention hit like a drug. Or, more precisely, like the first bad hit of something new and untested: Carmine's form spasmed, the paragraphs of his pseudo-flesh stretching and then snapping back under the onslaught of curated attention. Where the ring lights hit directly, the script-skin blistered and peeled, revealing patches of void beneath—pure, unwritten space, hungry and cold.

Cass whooped, "Get his good side!" and the ring of Modernisers closed in, every camera tracking and tracing Carmine's outline. For the first time since the world had learned to fear him, Carmine tried to hide, curling his body, turning away, raising an arm as if the collective stare would scald.

Vincent let himself smile—a real, ugly one, full of all the years of passive aggression he'd banked for this moment. "Keep the lights on him!" he bellowed. "Drown him in his own press!"

Aurelia snapped her fingers, and the entire squadron pivoted to full "engagement mode." Phones held overhead, they started broadcasting—some on TikTok, some on Instagram, a handful on whatever ephemeral platform Cass had designed for maximum narrative disruption. The feeds flooded the Archive, bouncing Carmine's image around the domed walls, each new angle introducing a different filter: one made his teeth sparkle like a toothpaste ad, another gave his eyes a demonic red, a third inverted his palette entirely, turning him into a negative of himself.

The Archive reacted with pure disgust. Rows of shelving shook, sending rivulets of loose ink pouring from the edges. The spines of ancient ledgers flexed, buckled, then tore apart, as though the attention itself was contagious, a prion that infected the very substance of the place. Footnotes, stripped from the margins, twitched on the floor like dying insects.

Carmine screamed—not the booming, aria-of-doom scream of a classic villain, but the shrill, human shriek of someone in real, abject pain. His body juddered, every sentence on his skin vibrating in place, then erupting in a spray of raw, broken clause. He tried to summon the narrative shield again, hands weaving sigils in the air, but the Modernisers just followed, ring lights adjusted, cameras close, commentary running in a constant, mocking patter.

"Who wore it better?" Nyx deadpanned to their stream, zooming in on Carmine's unravelling shoulder.

"Follow for more chaos," Cass added, toggling between selfie cam and the live carnage, his face lit with the unholy joy of a child let loose in a fireworks factory.

Aurelia, never outdone, raised both arms and pivoted, giving her followers a three-sixty tour of the suffering. "If you're just joining," she intoned, "we're live from the Archive, and this is what happens when you mess with the Moderniser Collective."

Her voice held the hard, crystalline edge of someone who had absolutely planned for this moment. "Smash that like button if you want to see what happens next."

Vincent almost pitied Carmine. Almost.

Carmine scrabbled backwards, leaving a slick trail of ink and ruined text behind him. The patches of void on his body spread—where once the stories had crammed every inch, now the gaps yawned, swallowing even the script around them. His face flickered between identities, cycling through every version of himself that had ever existed, but none lasted more than a frame or two.

The Modernisers pressed in. The ring lights, wielded now as clubs, struck Carmine's arms and shoulders, burning away the last resistance. "Say cheese," Cass jeered, and the word "cheese" actually appeared, in Comic Sans, across Carmine's brow for a split second before dissolving in a fit of digital static.

The Archive rebelled. Manuscripts flew from the walls, pelting the crowd with a hail of hostile, screaming ephemera. A flurry of legal briefs caught Aurelia in the chest, but she batted them aside with an indifferent flick of the wrist. Cass ducked as a hardbacked codex sailed over his head, then caught the next one and used it as a makeshift shield. Nyx, multitasking like a champion, live-mixed a beat on a phone app while simultaneously ducking shuriken-shaped citation slips.

Vincent circled the perimeter, watching for an opening. Mrs Barley had fallen back, dragging Ren with her, both battered and spattered with blood and less pleasant fluids. Ren's Mark, glowed like a newly minted star, pulsing faster and faster as the spectacle reached its peak. Mrs Barley's eyes tracked the battle with a bureaucrat's cold detachment, but Vincent could see the telltale twitch at the corner of her mouth: she was loving every second.

Carmine tried to rally. He lifted his arms and, for a split second, the voids on his body aligned, forming a lens of pure nothingness that swallowed the next barrage of light. But the Modernisers just amped up the exposure, phones set to "sunburn," ring lights dialled to "retinal detachment." They streamed the collapse from every angle, and the crowd on the other side of the cameras—hundreds of thousands, now, maybe millions—fuelled the spectacle with their comments, emojis, and gleeful reposts.

Carmine's narrative cracked. The skin of his body tore open, not along the seams of sentence or story, but in ragged, organic fissures. From each gash, a whirlwind of abandoned plotlines screamed out, only to be caught by the ring lights and incinerated in the viral heat. Carmine's voice split into a dozen versions: the self-aggrandising, the pleading, the coldly rational, the sheerly desperate. All shrieked at once, a feedback loop of failed narratives.

Vincent took that moment, and only that moment, to step up to the dais.

He looked at Carmine, now a smoking latticework of stories and void, and said, "Any last words for your fans?"

Carmine tried to answer, but all that came out was a noise—like the world's worst modem handshake, or the final, dying gasp of an old, beaten dog.

"Thought not," Vincent said.

He turned to the Modernisers. "Finish it."

Aurelia pointed her phone, and the rest followed. They surrounded Carmine, every camera broadcasting, every comment section a tidal wave. The light, now a physical force, pressed Carmine flat to the dais, melting the remainder of his story into a puddle of ink and howling emptiness.

The Archive convulsed. The floors shuddered, the shelves collapsed, the rivers of ink boiled, then evaporated into a haze of pure, unrecoverable data loss. The memory of Carmine, once indelible, now struggled even to persist as a meme. Nyx, always the DJ, looped the dying moments on the stream, remixing Carmine's last words into a stuttered, unrecognisable hook.

Vincent glanced at Mrs Barley, then at Ren, then at the absolute bedlam around him.

He smiled.

It was nearly over.

The Modernisers, at Aurelia's barked command, closed ranks. They circled Carmine with military precision—though it was the precision of a sales team during Black Friday, not an army. Every ring light was now a searchlight, every phone a weaponised rumour. The Modernisers marched, stomped, and took their places, forming a perfect perimeter around the battered dais where Carmine cowered.

Aurelia raised her arms and, with the natural authority of someone who had once out-negotiated three rival agencies before breakfast, began to lead the crowd. "Boost the signal!" she shouted, voice echoing across the Archive. "If you want to see him go down, hit that like button! Make history with us!"

The line of Modernisers began a slow, ritualised chant—

something between a football song and a sacrificial hymn. It started small, but with every verse, their numbers grew: each echo bounced back as ten, each ten became a hundred, and soon the whole Archive trembled with the sound. Phones shook with the incoming notifications. The air was a live feed of hashtags, slogans, and calls to action, all funnelled directly at the shrieking nucleus of Carmine.

Cass was a blur of activity, switching between three devices, all running separate livestreams. "We're trending globally!" he shrieked, voice breaking in pure, unfiltered glee. "Number one in London, Paris and New York, number three worldwide!" The numbers rose faster than the Archive's walls could process; somewhere overhead, the very structure began to warp, stretching to accommodate the swelling audience.

Nyx, deadpan and perfectly attuned, cued up a choral bed of sound from their phone. Every beat landed in sync with the chant, each drop echoing the rhythm of a million scrolling thumbs. Between verses, they stitched in clips of Carmine's contorted face, re-looped and re-autotuned until the old man's shrieks became a meme in real time.

On the ground, the viral magic was literal: the more people watched, the less Carmine could defend himself. Every hashtag posted—#CarmineChallenge, #CouncilFail, #RewriteThe-Night—pinned another piece of him to the dais. The Archive's pages, no longer bound to their shelves, drifted down in a snow of hostile witness. Each page recorded a new humiliation, a fresh contradiction, a misquote so devastating that it struck Carmine physically, opening fresh wounds of raw, writhing script.

Carmine tried to fight back, but every time he opened his

mouth, a different version of himself spoke, none agreeing with the last:

"You don't understand—"

"This was never the plan—"

"History belongs to the victors—"

"It's a joke, a hoax, all of it—"

The contradictory voices layered, overlapped, and, in the viral amplification of the moment, cancelled each other out. It was the sound of a man outmoded by his own story, doomed to narrate his own irrelevance as the audience chanted for more.

Vincent, keeping one battered arm clamped across his gut, turned to Ren, who was hovering just behind Mrs Barley in the outer circle. The Mark on her arm had gone from blue to white-hot, leaking thin streams of vapour that fizzed and snapped in the air. Her face was a mask of pain, but her eyes—always the most alive thing in the room—were fixed on Carmine with a fanatic's clarity.

She said, "He's not just bleeding attention—he's starving for it."

Mrs Barley, who had acquired a fresh batch of anti-memetic stickers and plastered them across her own arms and neck, took one look at Carmine and nodded. "He's running out of script. If you have anything left, now is the time."

Vincent nodded for Ren to go.

She didn't hesitate. She pressed the Marked forearm to her chest, wrapped her other hand around it, and pulled. The pain was so immediate it blanked her vision, but she kept pulling, until the surface of her skin unzipped like wet paper and the Mark came away in her hand: not a tattoo, but a living, screaming spiral of text, brighter than a phosphor flare.

She looked at it—her own story, all the grief and anger and noise Carmine had written into her—and then she did the most logical, most Ren thing imaginable: she walked straight through the ring of Modernisers, dodged a swipe from Carmine's ruined hand, and slapped the Mark directly onto his chest.

It burned like a brand, sizzled against the void-skin, then burst into flame. Carmine's entire body went rigid, his eyes rolling back as the recursive feedback of prophecy and exposure hit all at once. The viral crowd saw it, loved it, and took the opportunity to meme it to hell.

Cass, never missing a beat, shouted, "Like and share to banish the darkness! Let's finish this bastard!"

The comments flooded in: "Best ARG ever," "CGI is INSANE," "Vincent Lupo is Daddy." Each comment landed like a punch. Nyx let the beat drop, and the entire Archive vibrated with the shared, giddy joy of a million strangers watching a bad guy get what he deserved.

Ren staggered back, but Mrs Barley caught her by the shoulders, steadying her.

Mrs Barley's turn.

She strode to the dais—now a shambles, ink pooling around the base, Carmine writhing and failing at the centre—and planted her umbrella tip in the stone with the full, bureaucratic authority of every Council notary who had ever lived and died by the paperwork. She clicked the ferrule, extending a silver spike, and pressed it into the dais with the certainty of an executioner's axe.

The effect was immediate. The ground cracked, fissures racing outward from the umbrella's point. Each fracture glowed, then erupted, white light fountaining through the Archive's floor like the upwelling of a buried sun. Manuscripts caught fire, the flames blue and clean, erasing every trace of Carmine's gospel with all the finality of a hard drive scrubbed at Ministry —of-Defence standards.

Carmine's last words were not a scream, or even a curse. They were a simple, desperate plea, voiced in every version at once:

"The story... must stay hidden..."

But it didn't.

It poured out of him—every secret, every atrocity, every lie and half-lie and carefully engineered omission. It streamed into the light, where the Modernisers' phones captured it, cut it, edited it, and sent it viral before Carmine had time to edit a single word. The last of his power, the narrative engine that had kept him running for centuries, was ripped out and consumed by the crowd.

He convulsed, shuddered, then, for a split second, reconstituted as the man he'd once been—tired, old, and alone. He looked at Vincent, and Vincent looked back, and for a moment neither of them said anything.

Then Carmine shattered. He broke into a million fragments, each one a story denied, a rumour disproved, a meme outlived. The pieces dissolved, absorbed by the Mark still burning at his heart.

Ren watched as the Mark—her Mark—ate the last of Carmine's story, then went out like a guttered candle. And with it, the pain in her arm stopped.

The Modernisers, having achieved virality, broke into celebration: selfies, hugs, impromptu dance parties. Nyx livestreamed the last moments, then shut off the feed and let the deck fall silent for the first time in hours. Cass ran a victory lap, then collapsed in a pile of ash and giggles.

Aurelia, always aware of optics, pulled Vincent and Mrs Barley in for a group shot, capturing the survivors against the backdrop of a ruined, but cooling, Archive. "History," she said, "belongs to the ones who write it. Or at least, the ones who know how to use a good filter."

Vincent looked around: Ren, exhausted but alive. Mrs Barley, already reloading her umbrella with fresh bureaucratic forms. The Modernisers, victorious in their own unique way. And, everywhere, the silence of a story that had finally, truly ended.

TWENTY-THREE

Back at Vincent's flat, reality reasserted itself as a combination of threadbare furniture, bad air freshener, and the ambient throb of the fridge trying not to die of neglect. The shock of normality was so abrupt that Vincent's first thought, after the tumble, was that he'd hallucinated the whole thing. Except for the blood—his own, and the memory of Carmine's. And the ink, which was still everywhere, even after three full-body wipe-downs with the least allergenic baby wipes money could buy.

Ren flopped onto the sofa, nearly dislocating Mrs Barley's shoulder in the process. She looked as though she'd just finished a triathlon in a hailstorm—her hoodie shredded to bandages, skin all pallor and bruising, eyes huge and unfocused. She cradled her left arm, the Mark now nothing more than a cauterised welt, angry red and faintly luminous under the apartment's lighting. The fingers of her right hand twitched, as if still conducting the feedback loop of prophecy gone to seed.

Vincent didn't trust his legs to support him, so he took the armchair by the window. He doubled over, elbows on knees, and retched quietly into a handkerchief. What came up was half blood, half the slick black ink of a printer dying somewhere deep in the NHS. He spat, wiped his lips, and for the first time since puberty, wondered if maybe a little less hunger would be a blessing.

The fridge compressor ticked over, drowning out the after-shocks of silence. Mrs Barley, having checked her own pulse (twice), snapped the remains of her umbrella closed and propped it gently against the radiator. The silver tip had bent into a backwards S, and the fabric was, in places, more absent than present. She regarded the weapon for a moment—either as a memory of service or a candidate for proper recycling—then turned her attention to the others.

"Report," Mrs Barley said, voice stripped of everything but muscle memory.

Ren raised her head, blinked, and muttered, "All present. All correct. All more or less still here."

Vincent glanced at Zara, who hovered above the carpet, a ghost even by the low standards of post-Carmine London. She had trouble maintaining shape: half her face faded in and out, the rest an impressionistic sketch of a smile. If she had any remaining strength, she spent it on the effort of not letting her hand pass through the furniture.

The four sat in a circle of after-battle quiet, as if the flat itself needed a minute to process what had just been extruded into it.

Vincent broke the lull. "How long do we have?" He wasn't sure if he meant before the world rebooted, or before he ran out of second chances.

Mrs Barley tapped her watch, then consulted the mobile, then the battered legal pad. "Time is currently holding," she said. "But only in the local sense. Globally—" She frowned, as if global time was a personal affront.

Ren reached up, peeled a flake of dried blood from her ear, and asked, "Does that mean we won?"

Mrs Barley considered. "We succeeded in preventing narrative recursion. Carmine is—" She hesitated, and Vincent noticed the wince, as if admitting to a murder one was supposed to regret. "Extinguished. Permanently. Zara saw to it."

Zara wavered, the effort of being seen costing her. "Did what editors do best," she slurred, voice running down like a battery. "Cut for clarity."

Ren tried to smile, but it looked like the muscle had forgotten its training. "You're a bloody hero, then."

Zara winked out, then back. "Can't spell hero without 'eulogy.' Or something. Give me a minute, I'll be funnier next time."

Vincent, feeling his insides try to pick a side between solid and liquid, leaned back. The movement sent a jolt of pain down his right side: the garlic burn had scabbed, but a shaft of sunlight from the window found its way to his cheek, and the patch sizzled instantly, leaving a smoking welt.

He jerked away, hissing.

Ren saw it, eyes snapping to his. "You're still—?"

He nodded, the motion making him woozy. "Apparently, old habits die hardest. Or not at all."

The Mark on Ren's arm glowed faintly, then faded. She looked down at it, running a finger along the scar.

"Does it hurt?" Vincent asked, mostly out of a perverse need to divert the attention away from himself.

"Not as much as it should," Ren replied. She looked at him again, closer this time, and the lines around her mouth set. "You're not coming back from this, are you?"

He didn't answer. He just looked at his hands—stained, callused, more stranger than self. He flexed them once, watching the tendons jump, and thought of all the things Carmine had tried to write into him. Maybe one day he'd learn to edit them out, but right now, it felt like every part of him was still arguing with the rest.

Mrs Barley, who had retrieved her notebook, began to write. She filled the page with dense, looping script—observations, conclusions, action items—her pen moving with a fluid, almost vengeful grace. It was the bureaucracy of recovery, a way to make sense of the madness by numbering it, footnoting it, and rendering it harmless through repetition.

Vincent watched, and felt something like envy.

On the sofa, Ren closed her eyes, shoulders shuddering as she exhaled. Her hand rested on the Mark's scar, but she didn't try to cover it. There was no more need for hiding: the secret was out, and, for once, the world hadn't ended.

Zara slumped sideways, one foot passing straight through the coffee table. "Told you," she whispered. "Good editors bleed."

Vincent grinned, despite himself. The sound was wet, but honest.

He waited for the world to reset, for the news to break, for the next idiocy to sweep the city.

But for now, he just let himself rest.

TWENTY-FOUR

The Council Chamber of the Court of Pale Affairs had weathered revolutions, schisms, a brief but memorable coup by the Vampires for Environmental Justice, and at least six pandemics—some viral, some ideological. But in the history of its stained-glass vault and moon-pocked limestone, nothing had ever punctured its composure quite like a Moderniser livestream.

At the centre of the chamber, a dozen crystal screens hung suspended above the ancient debating pit, each one tuned to a different corner of the Internet's collective shriek. The Archive battle replayed in an infinite loop, spliced and memed and hashtagged into a digital afterlife that made the Council's official Minutes read like a suicide note in Courier font. On the big feed, a freeze-frame of Carmine mid-collapse—his face flickering between villain and meme-template—had already accrued four million likes, two hundred thousand "scream" reactions, and a running commentary that swung between "vampires r real, I KNEW IT" and "CGI's getting wild these days lol."

Elder Mortimer Blackthorn perched at the apex of the debating pit, his robes stiff with starch and the kind of dignity you could only buy by outliving four centuries' worth of rivals. His colleagues fanned out on either side, forming a wall of bloodless, unamused faces—enough to unsettle anyone except those accustomed to the ritual humiliation of other people's ambitions. Blackthorn's eyes, sunk deep into his skull, flicked from screen to screen as though searching for a version of events that made him the winner.

Vincent, bandaged from eyebrow to ankle, watched the proceedings from a stone bench two steps below the Elder. The sightlines in the Chamber were strictly hierarchical: every seat down the line forced you to look up at your betters, and in this particular arrangement, Vincent was sandwiched between the Modernisers and the rest of what Mrs Barley had dubbed "the doomed alumni reunion." Ren sat at his right, pale but alive, her hand still wrapped in a sling and her eyes tracking every flicker of the screens. To his left, Mrs Barley clutched her handbag, face set in a way that had carried her through three previous regime changes.

The Modernisers stood as a block, as if by sheer proximity they could keep from being vaporised by the Council's combined gaze. Aurelia Voss looked the least bothered, her platinum hair so perfectly lacquered that the chamber's cold lighting seemed to bead and roll off it. Cass, beside her, was too busy texting what had to be the world's most viral victory lap to notice he'd torn a chunk out of his own hoodie in the Archive's final scramble. Nyx, as ever, hovered somewhere between sleep and transcendence, their eyes hidden behind mirrored shades but their ears tuned to every subharmonic in the chamber.

On the screens, the Carmine meme hit a new high: someone had deepfaked his final words to say, "If you agree that cats are cute. Don't forget to like and subscribe." The Council did not, as a rule, laugh, but the snort from the lower benches was unmistakable.

Elder Blackthorn silenced the room with a raised pinkie, the same gesture that once sent entire tribunals into catatonic submission. "We are gathered," he intoned, "to address the aftermath of what has been termed the Carmine Recursion Event." The screens behind him auto-captioned this as "#carminefail," which nearly cracked Mrs Barley's poker face.

"Let the record reflect," Blackthorn went on, "that the Modernisers'... intervention, while in violation of a dozen standing bylaws, did prevent total narrative collapse and the loss of mortal consensus reality."

Aurelia beamed, bowing with both hands as if she'd just nailed the sales task on a particularly difficult episode of *The Apprentice*. "It was a team effort," she said, aiming the smile at Vincent and Ren as though expecting them to join the group photo.

Vincent's left eyebrow raised itself over the bandage and muttered, "First time anyone called me a team player." Ren grinned, the motion barely controlled.

Cass piped in: "We've already spooled up the damage control. By tonight, trending will have shifted to conspiracy debates and there's a poll on which government minister is actually a spy working for the North Koreans." He sounded so proud of this that several council members had to check their notes for the correct facial response.

Nyx, not to be outdone, added: "We've scheduled a post-credits stinger for tomorrow night. Get ahead of the story, or the story gets ahead of you."

Mrs Barley scribbled this verbatim into her pad, then leaned over to Vincent. "You realise," she murmured, "that if the Modernisers get Council commendation, every two-bit vampire with a Wi-Fi signal is going to think they're a strategic asset."

Vincent shrugged. "You can always threaten to ban their accounts."

Mrs Barley snorted, and for a moment the two were united in the cold comfort of knowing that no disaster was so great it couldn't be made worse by a committee.

At the far end of the dais, the council's oldest living member —a woman so desiccated she could have been carved from migraine—leaned forward. "If it pleases the House," she croaked, "we might consider a formal statement. The public requires an explanation, or at the very least a reliable villain." She shot a withering glance at the Modernisers. "Preferably one with a shorter attention span than Mr Lupo."

Vincent offered a mock salute.

The next twenty minutes were a slow-motion car crash of ritual and passive aggression. The Council drafted, amended, and re-drafted an official narrative, each round more baroque than the last. They attempted, with decreasing subtlety, to pin the whole affair on "rogue agents," then "cultural sabotage," then, in a last-ditch flail, "the regrettable rise of disruptive technology." But the Modernisers, now emboldened, batted every charge aside with a mixture of prepared statements and the raw, viral evidence of their own livestreams. By the end of the debate, it was clear that the best the Council could hope for was to avoid being memed out of existence before tea.

Ren, watching the fireworks, nudged Vincent in the ribs. "They're terrified of us."

He watched Blackthorn's quill hover over the official motion, the Elder's hand trembling just enough to betray the cost. "They should be," Vincent whispered. "We're the only thing keeping them from being last week's news."

Mrs Barley, sensing the moment, began a fresh note: "Moderniser threat not tactical. Existential. Recommend adoption of disruption protocols or compulsory influencer onboarding." Vincent bit his tongue to avoid a laugh, which earned him a glare from Mrs Barley and a sidelong smile from Ren.

Aurelia, eyes fixed on the Elder, called out, "So, are we Council now?" The room recoiled. The screens froze on her face, high cheekbones and shark eyes, the next meme already assembling itself in the data centre of the world's id.

Blackthorn set down the quill. The official, hand-calligraphed commendation rolled into existence at the centre of the dais, its wax seal bleeding a little more red than necessary.

"In recognition of services rendered to the Compact and the greater narrative, the Council acknowledges the Modernisers as... 'useful assets' in the ongoing containment of the supernatural." The words hung in the air like a bad smell.

Cass fist pumped. Nyx executed a dab so lazy it could have been performed from the grave.

Aurelia beamed, then, with the grace of a seasoned pro, offered her hand to Vincent. He considered it, then shook, squeezing just hard enough to remind her which one of them had the longer fangs.

Ren, emboldened, winked at Cass, who blushed so fast he nearly short-circuited his own phone.

Mrs Barley clicked her pen, then straightened her skirt. "Shall we adjourn before they start asking for a quote?"

The Council, released from the obligation to pretend they enjoyed their glimpse of the future, shuffled out in a dignified panic. Elder Blackthorn lingered, gaze burning a hole through the back of Vincent's skull.

"History's first vampire PR win," Vincent muttered, just loud enough for Mrs Barley and Ren to hear. "We're doomed."

Mrs Barley shot him a look so sharp it could have drawn blood, but Ren just snickered and said, "At least you'll be trending."

Vincent, for the first time all morning, allowed himself a smile.

He followed the others out, the weight of a thousand failed prophecies replaced, for once, by the lighter burden of victory.

Vincent's flat looked like the murder scene in an Ikea catalogue: bloodless but not bloodless, furniture scattered in dramatic agony, and every reflective surface still edged with the blue afterglow of a haunting. The fridge, having lost its will to live somewhere in the night, hummed in a minor key. The ring lights were gone, replaced by a single battered lamp held together with gaffer tape and stubbornness, its shade so singed that it projected Rorschach blots onto the walls.

Vincent had staked out the sofa, more out of injury than preference. Bandages ran up his arms and around his throat, and the only reason his right ear remained attached was because Ren had pressed it back on and threatened him with a kebab skewer if he so much as twitched during the glue job. The garlic burn had scabbed, then blistered, then scabbed again, and he'd stopped bothering to check whether the scars were healing. Some wounds, as Ren put it, were a lifestyle.

Ren herself lay sprawled at the other end of the sofa, hoodie zipped to the chin, hands tucked under her knees. Her eyes never quite settled, constantly flickering between her phone (which she hadn't charged in sixteen hours), the TV (permanently muted and locked to the news), and her own left arm, where the Mark was now just a faint, angry scar. Every so often she'd run her thumb over the skin, then snatch it away as if expecting the story to restart.

At the kitchen table, Mrs Barley typed. Her hands, quick and merciless, hammered the battered laptop. The scent of lemon-scented cleaner and instant coffee drifted from the sink, locked in a perpetual stalemate with the staleness of a room that hadn't been opened to the world in months.

Zara drifted. Sometimes she was visible, standing in the doorway as if weighing whether to join in or start her own haunting. Sometimes she was just a shimmer in the corner of the eye, an afterimage that left the hairs on your arms standing up even when you'd seen her die twice. Today, she favoured corporeal, but it was the kind of corporeal that looked seconds from being uploaded to the cloud.

"Is this what a win feels like?" Ren asked, breaking the silence. Her voice was hoarse, as if she'd spent the night screaming at a football match or the collapse of a minor universe. "Because I kind of want my money back."

Vincent grunted. He'd spent most of the morning trying to piece together what the Council's official version of events would look like, and how best to subvert it before they tried to nail him to the cross of "complicity." So far, the only good news was that Carmine's name had dropped from the trending tags, replaced by the minor scandal of a Tory MP caught sexting a Moderniser bot.

"Could be worse," Vincent said, rolling a shoulder and wincing at the sound of dried bandage snapping. "Could be dead."

Mrs Barley, who had never let existential dread interfere with a deadline, said, "If you are dead, please advise so I can reassign your tasks. Otherwise, you're due at Moderniser HQ at twenty hundred."

Vincent let his head flop back against the sofa. "I don't want to see another smartphone in my life. Thought I earned a promotion."

Mrs Barley didn't look up. "Technically, you're a person of interest in four ongoing investigations. It's better if you're visible."

"Visible," echoed Zara, voice thin as tracing paper. "That's one way to put it."

Ren snorted. "At least you're not trending as #VincentThe-Incel. Cass is already selling T-shirts."

"I'm not even an incel," Vincent protested. "I've had sex. Loads of it. Just not... recently."

This, finally, cracked a smile from Ren. "If it helps, the fans think you're secretly pining for Carmine."

Vincent made a noise halfway between a laugh and a growl. "I'd rather drink bleach."

Zara floated over, face sharpened with mischief. "If you're out of bleach, I've got a backup plan. You, me, and a night of 'educational' livestreams. We'll have the mortals begging for a return to Love Island."

He raised an eyebrow. "Are you even allowed on TikTok anymore?"

She shrugged, shoulders blurring. "Only in parental advisory mode."

Mrs Barley finished a paragraph and closed her laptop with a snap. "If you're quite done wallowing, we have work to do. The Council expects a full report by end of day, including recommendations for containment."

Vincent blinked. "Containment of what? Carmine's gone."

Mrs Barley's eyes gleamed. "Not Carmine. Us. The Modernisers. The public. Anyone who thinks the world is more interesting with vampires in it."

Ren set her jaw. "Are they going to try and memory-wipe the planet again?"

Mrs Barley shrugged. "Unlikely. The Archive was a one-off. But they will deploy 'soft reset' measures—rumour, disinformation, algorithmic distraction." She regarded Vincent over the rim of her reading glasses. "You'll be on the front line. Enjoy."

The silence grew roots.

Zara, still only half-there, sat on the arm of the sofa and nudged Vincent's good leg with her own. "Don't let them stick you in another basement with a tape recorder. You deserve to be part of the story."

He rolled his eyes. "I just want a quiet life."

She grinned. "Then you picked the wrong afterlife, mate."

There was a knock at the door. It didn't sound like the old, tentative tap of a pizza delivery, or the frenzied, police-battering-ram kind. It was, unmistakably, the knock of a bureaucrat: three sharp raps, a pause, then one more for emphasis.

Mrs Barley answered. A man in a charcoal suit stood in the hall, hair slicked flat, eyes so wide apart it looked like he'd been assembled in a dark room by someone reading the manual upside down. He carried a plastic document wallet in both hands, arms straight out, as if terrified of contaminating either himself or the recipient.

"Council delivery," he said, voice tuned to exactly the level of Just Doing My Job.

Mrs Barley signed for the folder, flicked through the contents, and snapped it closed. "More stakeouts," she announced, dropping the file onto the coffee table. "More Modernisers. More 'containment.' Vincent, you're back on fieldwork. Ren, you're with him. Zara—" she paused, then, with the faintest tilt of the lips, "keep being yourself."

The messenger vanished. Zara whistled, long and low. "Saved the world, get sentenced to binocular duty. Classic."

Ren snatched up the file, flipped through the first ten pages, and snorted. "They even spelled your name wrong. Twice."

Vincent scanned the assignments. "They've paired us with Modernisers for every round. Are they hoping we'll rub off on them, or the other way round?"

Mrs Barley reclaimed her laptop and umbrella, as if these

were the tools that would see her through the coming plague of idiocy. "If you're not dead in a week, I'll update your performance review."

Zara, seeing the darkness in Vincent's face, leaned in until their noses nearly touched. "You don't have to do this. You can run. Hide. Move to Birmingham. They'll never look for you there."

He smirked. "Wouldn't last a week in Birmingham. I'd combust on the ring road."

She grinned, her outline flickering to a bright, electric blue for the first time that day. "You're all right, Lupo. Even if you're Council's least favourite bastard."

"Someone's got to be," he said, and for a moment, he felt almost normal.

Ren closed the file and tossed it onto the heap of half-eaten curry containers. "So, what's next?"

Vincent reached for the remote, flicked through three channels, then set the TV to an ancient documentary about the collapse of the Habsburg Empire. "Stakeouts, obviously," he said, scratching his chin with a bandaged hand. "But first—kebabs."

The others nodded, the kind of silent agreement you only got from people who'd survived something together.

And as the night wound down, and Zara faded in and out with the stories on the screen, Vincent allowed himself the luxury of believing, just for a minute, that maybe the world was worth a second draft.

Keep reading the **Fang & Loathing Trilogy** with **Book 3: Rewrite the Dead**

NOTE FROM THE AUTHOR

Hi,

Thanks so much for reading *The Stakeout Diaries*!

It was a lot of fun to write. I truly hope it was an entertaining read.

If you enjoyed the book, I would be incredibly grateful if you'd be so kind as to leave a review.

Reviews really help authors for a number of reasons, not least, providing feedback on what readers like and improving visibility of the book on online retail sites.

Thanks in advance and I look forward to reading your thoughts.

Jon

ABOUT THE AUTHOR

Jon Smith is the bestselling author of more than 50 books for children, teens, and adults. His books have sold over half a million copies and have been published in seven languages.

In addition to writing books, Jon is an award-winning screenwriter and musical theatre lyricist and librettist with productions at the Birmingham Hippodrome, Belfast Waterfront, London's Park Theatre and PJPAC, Kuala Lumpur.

A father of four, he lives near Liverpool with his wife and their two school-age children.

When he grows up he'd like to be a librarian.

www.jonsmith.net

x.com/jonsmith_author

instagram.com/jonsmith_author

goodreads.com/jonsmith_author

amazon.com/author/jonsmith

facebook.com/authorjonsmith

MAILING LIST

Want to receive advance information about future publications?

Fancy exclusive access to freebies, special offers and bonus material?

Feel that your life isn't complete without Jon's monthly musings about writing, reading and publishing?

There's a solution! Sign up today to Jon's mailing list:

https://jonsmith.net/mailing-list

THE FANG & LOATHING TRILOGY

BALKON
media

www.ingramcontent.com/pod-product-compliance
Lightning Source LLC
Chambersburg PA
CBHW050609190726
48283CB00007B/2339

9 781916 970199